Love Sex Death

Short stories

by

Howard Evans

Cover design by Marie Tilbert
Skull designed by Ajipebriana / Freepik

Double Dorje
34 Marley House
London, W11 4DJ
UK

ISBN: 978-1916201224

Love Sex Death

Author's note

Although they have benefitted from recent rewriting, some of these stories were conceived a long time ago, in the days before mobile phones, in the days when smoking was permitted everywhere. I left them like that, as stories from a very different time.

Magic bus

How was it decided - which one of us should die? Did you know I was lying there beside you, terrified, unaware of the blood seeping from your wounds? Did you think of me then, the one who woke beside you on the roof, the one who was woken by your nightmare screams?

Did you remember my words of reassurance? Were they lies then as I said them, or did they only turn to lies in the midst of the violence? Did you remember my arms around you - my kiss? I've always wondered if you took my place or would death have found you wherever it was you were.

It was years before I could talk about it, even then only as a series of facts, like the fact of birth, lived but not remembered, or lived and then forgotten. I still gather the fragments, looking for the whole story amongst those pieces of memory.

I don't remember you in Tehran, but of course you were there, with the rest of us in the Amir Kabir, the only hotel that still welcomed us travellers in that city in chaos, that city suspended between celebration and sudden death. Outside the hotel we tried to explore the city, tried to move invisibly through the crowds, tried to avoid the men in white shirts who pushed against us with their guns.

I wanted to tell them, "We're happy for you. We're glad the Shah is gone. We supported Khomeini in Paris."

But it wasn't true. We were not on their side. This wasn't our revolution. We were idle travellers from the west with our loose morals and shabby clothes. We were not invited to this celebration. Our names were not on the list of those destined to flee or die.

That was where my fear began, in the Amir Kabir, where the world first became a hostile place. Perhaps I talked with you at that time, shared my fear, shared the rumours. Our embassies simply told us not to go but our drivers reassured us, told us that Afghanistan was fine.

When we reached Herat, we all knew we'd got it wrong, yet none would dare to say. We sat on the hotel roof in a shattered town, walked amidst the ruins of its walls, listened to the sound of gunfire in the distance. At night, soldiers arrived to protect us, installed a machine-gun at every corner. We slept together in that protected space, under the stars, silent with our fears, none of us willing to fracture the pretence. Nobody mentioned the shooting. Nobody mentioned the heavy guns and the young soldiers who stained that starry night.

Nobody mentioned their fear until you cracked the night with your scream and told me, as the day broke over the hills, of your death.

By then there was nowhere else to go. To return to the border with Iran was as frightening as going on, and the drivers told us again there was nothing to fear. These were their friends, they said. These were their brothers, they said. They had travelled this road many times before.

We smoked together, you and I, and drank tea with boiled sweets jammed in our cheeks. I don't remember what I said. Perhaps I just repeated the words of the driver. Perhaps I just raised my closed fist and waved it in the air, mimicking the missing fingers of his hand. I hadn't had your dream.

Later, I walked in the streets of Herat, walked again in the ruins. Still nothing of the destruction made sense. Nothing in the vague looks of the locals made sense. I lingered. I wanted to linger forever. I wanted to miss the bus, to stay in this shell of a town, to drink tea on the hotel roof, under the protection of the gunners.

I finally joined our little crowd at the bus, joined the huddle cramming bags into its belly - this old bus, this old wreck of a bus that had long since lost the magic it seemed to have when it arrived in that dirt yard in Istanbul. We were silent in that crowd, unable to look at each other, daring not to catch each other's eyes, in case we broke the spell.

I'll never know, but now I'm sure, each one of us felt the fear. Each one of us felt anticipation of something awful, and each one of us remained complicit in the silence, a silence broken only once by your nightmare scream.

What made you take my place? Why then, in all those days of travel, did you take that place, up there, up front with the driver? I remember the moment's indignation, an indignation that dispatched my fear, where fear was replaced by expectation of the drive into the mountains.

What was it that dispelled my indignation, made me concede my seat to you? Magnanimity? Generosity? Yielding? But yielding to what? Did I yield to your fate or yield my fate to you?

I took your place in the middle of the bus and watched as scared young soldiers took positions in the aisle. I watched as the bus set off beyond the town, beyond the long convoy waiting by the roadside, beyond the armoured cars and soldiers waiting with the trucks.

I never saw what stopped us. I assumed a roadblock, rocks, or men with guns. You must have seen it all from where you sat. For me, it took a while to understand. I still see the little hole of light that appeared above me in the roof. I still see the hole and crack beside me in the window. I still see the moment when the guy in front was killed, his head split open with a bullet. I still hear his girlfriend's cries, muted by disbelief.

Perhaps you were already hit. Perhaps those first screams were your screams. It was the screams that made it real, that made us all fall to the floor. It was the screams that made us realise that the air was filled with death.

Someone must have dragged you to where we lay but I don't remember you arriving. I just remember time slowed down, my back braced in expectation of a bullet, my eyes searching for explanation from other eyes that searched, and all the time the screams and the crack, crack, crack.

Some amongst us must have seen it all. Perhaps the Dutch guy, an army medic who helped the wounded, or the Swiss guy who turned the bus around and drove us back to Herat, or our drivers who leapt off into a hail of bullets. I never even asked them.

I only saw the mess as we drove back to town, when we finally dared to raise our heads from the bloody floor. That's when I saw you, still lying on the floor, your skin pale and the light receding in your eyes. I had no words for you, no words of reassurance, no arms to hold you, no kiss to wet your cheek. You were still alive when we reached the hospital and they carried you from the bus. I had to climb the seats to avoid your blood congealing on the floor, afraid to step in it as if to step in you.

You were taken in with the others, the dead or dying or wounded. The rest of us were left confused and aimless. You died soon after and you never saw those long strange days.

It seemed like weeks before we left - weeks living in the hotel courtyard, surrounded by walls and soldiers. Weeks walking the broken streets, taking our turn visiting our wounded friends.

The doctors reassured us, told us of the thousand wounds they'd treated. They told us of the tanks and jets that destroyed their town. They told us of this secret war that the world refused to see. In its midst we lived our half-life, amongst a people who were both our enemies and our friends, never sure if our voice was louder alive or dead.

You never saw those aimless days we passed nor witnessed the silence that we shared. You never saw those slow days in which nothing happened, days wished away without an aim. You never saw the drivers return, bullets dug from their flesh, wounds made good, nor witnessed our silent looks of sympathy and accusation. We all needed each other then and the need was stronger than the loathing. And yet, what we needed most we could not find. There was no one there to tell our story to. We were abandoned to a people who were abandoned by the world. Our story had no more value than theirs. I never counted the days nor knew how many weeks they made and, even now I sometimes wonder if I really lived that time. I have only snippets of memory to tell me I was there at all. I remember days passed drinking tea with shopkeepers who no longer had the heart to sell, days watching the baker hook flat loaves from his fiery oven deep inside the earth, days watching the miller's hooded camel on its endless journey around its cave, days waiting at the bed-side in the hospital for our friends to live or die.

In the evenings we sat together round a fire in the garden, eating bread and lamb, scorched by the flames. We shared a hookah filled with hashish - black resin pressed from powdery pollen in the fat hands of dealers from the south. In those clouds of oily, woody smoke we found our times of peace, when the sound of gunfire receded in our thoughts and our friendship of fear gave way to the friendship of the simple life survived.

I never knew who organised the plane, how it was that one day, suddenly, without expectation, we were leaving. Your body lay amongst the others, packed with our bags inside the hold. You never saw the flight over the mountains to Kabul, the deep blue lakes of Band-e-Amir. You never saw that other frightened city where we all split up and went our separate ways.

I guess your body was sent home to your family in France, to a family who, like mine, like me, like you, like all the others, never expected for us to walk into someone else's war.

The cell

Only two spiritual practices were given in the monastery. They were walking and washing one's clothes. In truth, although they were received, he was not sure it was quite right to say they were given. Nothing had actually been given since the day he arrived. He had never seen another soul since the young boy showed him to his cell. It was more as if these practices were discerned from the ancient stone walls that contained him. He wasn't sure how long it was since he had been sent to this place; he kept no record of time.

He had been living in a large canvas tent on the edge of the town. He lived with a Tibetan family who ran a restaurant selling momo, little steamed dumplings of either meat or mixed vegetable, and chang, an illegal rice beer which they brewed in large earthenware pots, hidden under a table at the entrance to the tent. During the day he washed dishes and vegetables and helped the children carry provisions from the market. At night he was free to eat momo and drink chang.

Sometimes, he was joined by an old lama who would sit beside him in silence. When the lama came, they were served a clear liquid which separated out on top of the milky chang. This drink had a potency similar to whiskey. Chang was more like weak beer.

He loved the silent drunkenness of the lama. He was the best drinking partner; his drunkenness was not confused with words.

One night the lama turned to him and said, "Tomorrow you leave - go here."

The lama handed him a scrap of paper with a tiny map drawn in pencil. He folded the map into his pocket and thanked him. That was all the lama ever said to him.

In the morning he packed his few possessions, thanked the family and left. He followed the dirt track into town and opened the map to find his bearings. The map led him past the many temples built by Buddhist nations of the world, and into a part of the town he had never visited before.

He arrived at an old stone wall with a wooden door set into it. He was greeted by a boy and led through a passage that ran along the wall to his cell. His cell was a tiny stone room, barely twice the size of the wooden bed it contained. On the bed was a thin rolled palliasse and two folded sheets. The room had a door and a small window which opened onto a courtyard garden.

He made the bed and lay down. The stillness was dreadful after the vibrancy of life with the Tibetans. After a short while he got up and stuck his head outside the door. A jug of water and some fruit and bread had been left there. He'd heard nothing.

He took the supplies into his room and lay down again. As he lay there, he became acutely aware of the agitation of his body. He couldn't find his comfort.

He decided to move the bed. The grating of its wooden legs against the stone floor disturbed him intensely as it reverberated against the silence of the room. He abandoned the plan and, with a final committed scrape, he shoved the bed back to the place it belonged. He stood for a moment in the centre of his cell. He noticed the shortness of his breath.

He deepened his breathing, slowed it down. Now it was too slow, too laboured, he could hear the excess tension in the muscles of his chest. He discovered that as he breathed, so his cell breathed with him. The discovery excited him and he started to play. He tried breathing more slowly. He tried different patterns. He tried holding his breath for a second, for two seconds, then four then eight. He tried exhaling fully and holding his breath as before. Once, by chance, when he stopped trying and his breathing became natural, he felt the atmosphere of his cell change. It alarmed him until he realised the profound beauty of the change. In the moment of noticing he lost the beauty. He could hear his agitation again.

He was tired from his efforts and lay down to rest. He fell asleep. He was woken by a single sound. He didn't know if it came from a gong or a bell.

In the quietness of just waking he listened to the sound. He could hear it expanding across the courtyard outside his window, contracting as it passed through the window into his cell. He heard harmonics as the sound touched surfaces of the room, fragmented, bounced momentarily back on itself, reformed into a completeness that defined his room, his bed, his body on the bed.

He noticed a response like a breath from everything touched by the sound. He noticed that everything was changed by the sound, minutely changed but forever different. As his surroundings settled into their new shape, he remembered his breathing. He discovered a rhythm that suited the room. It was a natural rhythm but it didn't come naturally. It asked that he try not too hard nor too little. To stay with that rhythm was like balancing on a wire. By lowering his centre of attention, from his head to his body, the balancing became less wobbly. Lowering his centre of attention was also like balancing on a wire. It called for a new kind of awareness, to avoid becoming too light or too heavy.

His efforts were lost in an urge to move, to leave his cell, to walk. He jumped out of bed and his clumsy movement resounded back on him from the walls. Now everything was different; even his movements affected his surroundings. His tension and clumsiness bounced back as a dissonant noise that disturbed him. He remembered the experiment with his breathing.

He lowered his centre of attention as he stood in the room. He became aware of a pulse in the air. He was not sure if he heard it or felt it. It arose from somewhere between sense and sensation. He knew it was the pulse of the cell at rest. He found a place in his body that corresponded to the pulse.

It was as if the cell became a metronome, a silent metronome. From within his body was an answer to the rhythm it gave. He tried to move and keep a sense of the rhythm. It was difficult. Each movement affected the rhythm. It was like dancing with a partner. He had to keep a sense of himself, of the movement of his body, of the pulse in his body, a sense of the room, of the space around him, of the pulse in the air. Every moment was different to the last. Every moment created afresh from the last. He felt alive, searching for the movement called for.

Now he saw that his movements were not his own, that there was a call from the room that asked for a response from within him. There was a constant search for the balance between what was asked for and what he could give. He started to walk and found that every step was like a meditation. Every step called for a new balance, a search for the right moment when his foot could touch the ground and the ground reached up to receive his foot. He was reminded of pushing a swing door, of catching the door as it swung back, of finding the precise moment when he could connect with its motion, and send it back without force.

As he walked from his cell and back towards the door, he found brief moments when something really connected - moments when, as with his breathing, he let go of the effort. They were moments when his sense of himself expanded, when he was no longer in control, no longer trying to do, when his body was walked and his body was breathed.

In those moments there was peace, free from trying, free from effort, free from worry, and yet contained within that peace was his agitation, his grasping, his trying, waiting for the moment when he would forget and they could seize him back.

He turned past the door and reached the courtyard garden. It was a small space contained by two walls and two arcades. Two diagonal paths cut across it and the four triangles so formed were delineated by hedges of box. Within each triangle were bushes of fragrant and aromatic herbs that offered new smells with each step. The garden was open to the sky which was framed like a living picture.

He stopped and rested at the edge of the path, listening to himself, to the shape of the courtyard, to the life of the plants. As he rested, he felt the new pulse, the pulse of the garden and courtyard and sky. He felt his anxiety returning, his body tightening, his breath shortening. He lost connection with the pulse and with himself. He wanted to turn and leave, to abandon this life and return to the tent. He could no longer find what was needed.

In the midst of his chaos, the tensions of his body and the tangle of his thoughts, he felt a call. Stillness called and supported him. He knew he had only to try, that he would be helped. He found his centre, found his own pulse and stepped forward. Each step called for the same, a moment to connect, to receive and to give. Slowly he travelled the path.

At the end of the path he passed through a space in the walls to a small contained yard. There was a porcelain toilet tray set in the floor with a hole for the waste and two raised ellipses for feet. Opposite the toilet was a large bathing tub built out of stone. A constant flow of clear water poured from a brass spigot set in the wall. Everything was spotlessly clean. The only sign that anyone else had been here was the slight wearing down of a block of soap that sat on the edge of the tub.

He undressed to relieve himself and to bathe in the water. He knew he would not be disturbed; this time was his own, this place was his for now.

Back in his cell he lay on his bed, listening to the pulse, giving himself to it, allowing himself to be drawn to that place with no time, no expectation, just quiet potential. From across the courtyard garden, from the little bathing yard, he heard a sound, a new rhythm. This was not a rhythm of this place, of the walls nor the structure. This was a rhythm made from the sound of washing clothes.

He could hear the sound of the fabric held beneath the spigot, absorbing its fill of water. He could hear the sound of the soap applied to the fabric. He could hear the sound of wet and soapy fabric pounded against the stone of the bath. The sound was not intrusive - it belonged, it harmonised with the bath and the soap and the stone and the building. It was an active improvisation, man and nature, doing and being done.

As he allowed the sound to mingle with him, he could hear the subtle changes, when the fabric needed more water or more soap. He could hear the sound of the water as it carried away the grime. He could hear the moment of clean, when no more was required, when the washer stopped the rhythm, wound the fabric into a coil, squeezed out the water and shook the fabric in the breeze.

Now he could only hear the sound of the monastery, that slow reference pulse, and yet he now knew that hidden within that pulse, blending with it, was another person - cleaning the bathing area, gathering things, walking across the diagonal that cut through the courtyard garden. Although he knew this was happening, there was no sound to betray the movements taking place except for one moment, when the person lost the connection and appeared for a second, emerged from a secret place contained within the rhythm of the space, and then was gone, invisible again.

He realised from this that there were others like him. They were like planets, each set in their motion. Each with their own orbit, their own speed, their own time, their own atmosphere. Each had their time to wake up, to walk, to bathe and to wash clothes. Each maintained the overall rhythm, and yet none were free from it. Each was invisible to the others, and yet each carried the responsibility of maintaining the rhythm for the others.

He deepened his listening, becoming aware of the moment when one of his invisible colleagues would lose the connection and appear. He realised that the others were listening too, holding the connection with the pulse, supporting the person in movement. He realised too that whenever he set off on his journey, from his cell, down the corridor, across the diagonal path through the garden, the others were listening for him, holding the pulse so that when he forgot, when he suddenly appeared, he could find his connection again.

One day, as he sat in his cell, he perceived a newcomer. He heard the agitation of thoughts, jarring with the quiet of the walls. He heard the stiffness and clumsiness of movement. He heard a bed scrape against stone and the discomfort of a body lying on the bed. He felt the unease enter his room and challenge his poise. He felt the call of responsibility and accepted. He sat silently on his bed and allowed himself to be drawn back, to the quiet, to his place in this structure.

He knew that throughout this place, there were others like himself, invisible, unseen, receiving a pulse, transmitting a pulse, supporting another who, like them had been sent to this monastery.

He knew now that his life was no longer his own and yet was more his own than ever before. He knew that in giving himself, he received himself afresh, dying and being reborn, moment by moment.

Now he would wake before the sound of the bell. Now he knew it was a bell. Now he could hear the moment before impact, the moment when a log suspended by four silk cords was drawn back.

He could hear the moment of preparation. He could hear the moment of release. He could hear the journey of a log through the air and he could hear the moment as wood met bronze. Now he could hear one side of the bell absorb the impact. He could hear the force distribute evenly throughout the form of the bell, for the bell was made by a master. He could hear the intake of air and the wave of expulsion followed by another and another as ripples of fluid bronze pushed the air until it formed a sound.

Now he could walk and wash clothes. Now he could give without knowing to whom. Now he could receive without knowing from where. Now he knew his time to move and his time to be still. Now he knew his place.

He awoke. It was earlier than usual. He eased himself from his bed to the floor and slowly walked from his room, measuring each step in turn according to the rhythm given. Instead of turning right as usual, he turned left and walked along the corridor. He passed many open doors, and knew it was not for him to look inside.

At the end of the corridor he turned left and found himself in a long arcade which he had only seen before from the other side - from the garden. His pace slowed, dictated by a deeper pulse than any he had encountered before. In the slowness of his journey he could feel that each arch was very slightly wider than the previous one and the space contained within the structure slightly grander than the previous one. Arch by arch he was slowing down until, toward the end of the arcade, he no longer had any sense of moving at all. It was now as if he were being moved, as if he had given himself over to another. In this state of near total abandonment, he found himself on a threshold notified by a thread of fine gold set into the stone pavement.

A question formed itself in his mind. "Are you ready?" He allowed the question to enter him, to become silent, to became a state. His body silently answered by stepping across the line. In front of him he saw the bell and, in line with his belly, the log suspended from four silk cords. He received the log into his hands and drew it back.

He prepared himself, waiting for the moment. The moment was given. He released the log.

He returned to his cell. There was no water jug, no bowl of fruit outside his door. He entered the cell. The palliasse was rolled up on the wooden bed. Two fresh sheets were folded on top. On the other end of the bed was some maroon fabric. He picked it up and it unfolded to reveal itself as a robe.

Still lying on the bed was an undershirt of vibrant saffron. He put them on and left his cell. When he reached the door to the street, he found it open. The young boy was waiting there. As he stepped through, the young boy raised his hands prayer fashion to his brow and bowed down. He turned and walked down the lane from the monastery until he reached the main street with its temples and hordes of milling tourists.

As he passed by, they were touched momentarily by the slight hush that remained in his wake. He reached the dirt track that led out of town to the refugee tents.

He entered the tent that he knew and, in one corner, saw a young tourist lost in his thoughts. He sat down beside him. Two glasses were brought of clear liquid from the top of the chang. They drank in silence together.

The dream

Originally published in TANK magazine, 1998

When the dream began, he was lying with his head towards the south-west, towards the wealth corner. He knew it was the wealth corner because Doctor Li had told him so. For this piece of information, Doctor Li had charged him £250. Dr Li charged him a further £50 for the brass spike he drove into the wall and for the crystal which he suspended by the window.

Doctor Li advised him to sleep with his head towards the wealth corner. This had been difficult. He had moved his bed from one side of the room to the other but, because of the orientation of his home, he was obliged to sleep diagonally across the mattress. His girlfriend didn't believe him when he told her needed to sleep diagonally because he was so tall. As far as she, could see nothing had changed. He hadn't grown any taller and his mattress seemed to be as long as it was the last time she slept on it. She was wise enough not to press him on the subject, he already had enough problems on his mind without her accusing him of lying. She accepted to take one of the remaining triangles and make the best of it.

There were times when he wanted to tell her the truth, but he was too embarrassed to tell her how he gave his last £300 to the old Chinese Feng Shui Master.

As the dream progressed, his body moved by degrees around the bed until his feet were pointing towards the wealth corner and his head towards the area of helpful people. This journey took more than an hour to complete but, finally, his body settled into its new position.

I know this is hard to believe, but the dream did continue without intermission throughout his body's journey and for another half hour beyond. The dream was in real-time and linear. It was not the usual multi-layered kaleidoscope of images and symbols typical of dreams. It was more akin to waking life in the clarity of its narrative. The dream was exact in its premonition. The location was as it would be. The people were as they would be. Even the weather was the warm grey drizzle which could not have been anticipated from the long dry spell which preceded it.

I watched him dream his dream night after night. I watched his body turn its half circle. I watched intently from within my dream, hoping for some clue as to what went wrong. When his dream was complete, I would wake up just as the sun-rise started to light my tiny room.

Each morning as I woke, I held my eyes closed for a moment, checking the dream, checking to see if something had changed, checking for something that might allow me to wake up and not be in this room.

Each morning I realised that the dream was the same. Nothing had changed and I would have to open my eyes to the same cold brick walls.

You probably realise something strange. Perhaps you wonder how it is that in my dream I can watch the dream of another. In truth I do not watch his dream, I only watch his body as he dreams. I only know his dream because he told it to me.

A month passed from the time when I started having the dream to the day I met him. It was a whole month before I knew what was happening in his inner world as his body turned on the bed. I started dreaming my dream the night after Dr Li had driven a brass spike into my wall. It was not in the wealth corner but in the area of fame. I paid Dr Li £50 for the spike and for the advice he gave me. Dr Li told me that I would gain the fame I craved but not for my acting. Dr Li told me that one day, quite soon, I would be walking in a part of the city I never usually visit. I would have an urge to go to a bar, to drink a glass of beer. In the bar I would meet a man. I would know it was the right man because he would tell me that he recognised me from somewhere. I would tell him that perhaps he had seen me on television but he would say no, that he had seen me in a dream. He would invite me to go with him to another bar, a quieter bar, where we could talk in private. I would go with him and he would tell me that he had been visited by an old Feng Shui Master. He would tell me what I had to do.

As predicted by Dr Li, I did find myself in a part of the city I never normally visit. I was called to a late casting and, after it was over, found myself in need of a glass of beer. I walked into a bar on route to the bus stop.

As I waited for my drink, a man came up to me and said that he recognised me from somewhere. I already knew the rest of the conversation and, resisting the temptation to be contrary, I followed it through to its proper conclusion. The man asked if I would join him at his table so we could talk in private. I told him he was supposed to ask me to come with him to another bar. He said he knew, but it was raining harder than he expected. Despite my misgivings, I joined him at his table near the cigarette machine.

The man told me he had been troubled by a recurring dream. In the dream, the world was at war. The scene was of awful carnage. In the middle of it, he saw himself shouting orders and directing the killing. He'd been scared by the dream and scared of the future it seemed to predict for him. He avoided anything which might lead him to that destiny. He immersed himself in a reclusive life, studying philosophical and religious texts. When his father was killed by an opponent's bullet in Lahore, he was introduced to Dr Li by the executor of his father's estate who knew of no other way to free him from the burden of his father's karma. Dr Li told him that he had only two choices. He could follow his heart and travel to Pakistan to avenge his father's death.

In so doing, he would connect with the destiny which he had already discerned from his dream. The alternative was this meeting and the events that would unfold from it. This choice would not only free him from his father's karma, it would also free his own son, already lodged in his girlfriend's womb, from the sins which his father had yet to commit.

The man told me that after Dr Li's visit, he started to have another dream. In this dream he meets me in a bar and asks me to join him for a drink. When we finish our drinks, he invites me to walk with him. We leave the bar and turn into an alley. A man appears from the shadows with a gun and shoots him dead. The killer turns the gun on me but it misfires. I wrestle the killer to the ground just as the police arrive.

Forensic evidence implicates the killer in a series of motiveless murders. A life sentence brings an early conclusion to what would otherwise become a reign of unchecked terror. I am hailed a hero and, through a karmic connection beyond my understanding, I guarantee the well-being of my progeny.

The man invited me to walk with him. I was still uncertain because of the change of plan due to the unexpectedly heavy rain. My companion assured me that it was the alley that counted, not the bar. I was further reassured when we stepped outside and the rain had become a warm grey drizzle. We turned into the alley and my awareness of events was curtailed by a sharp blow to the back of my head.

I regained consciousness on the concrete floor of a police cell where I was later charged with three counts of murder, evidenced by the gun found in my hand. My companion was dead and my assailant was commended for bravery by the court that sentenced me to life without parole. On my third day in prison I noticed a small brass button on the wall. After some hours of picking and scraping with my nails I withdrew a brass spike from the brickwork.

Two ends of the same stick

From STILL, published in 2019

"Let me share a story with you," she said.

"Many years ago, long before anybody thought of countries and borders there was a people who lived high up in the highest mountains. They lived in a stone village, hidden amongst the rocks and clouds. In the centre of their village was a great hall in which the people gathered. These people had been taught how to make paper and tan leather, how to sew and how to bind, how to make pigments and print, how to write and illustrate, how to make silver hasps and gold leaf. Around the walls of the great hall were shelves filled with the books they made - the greatest library on earth.

"A labyrinth of corridors and alleys surrounded the great hall, linking dormitories and kitchens, gardens and storerooms, water tanks, byres and stables. The people were divided into two types. There were those who enjoyed the crisp, thin mountain air and the beauty of the sky. These people maintained the village - building with stone, channelling water, keeping gardens, preparing food, teaching children, tending animals, listening, reading, writing, illustrating, story-telling and, when called upon, sitting in silence.

"The others preferred to live outside the stone village. In the spring they led the yaks and goats down from the mountain to graze them on fresh grass. They gathered wood to bring back to the stone village for the winter. As well as the yaks and goats, they also kept dogs that gifted their sense of smell and eagles that gifted their vision. These people liked to run. They ran as a tribe with their dogs and eagles, and gathered knowledge of the world to bring back to the scribes. They also ran because there was danger. There were people who travelled the land in hordes, who destroyed whole villages for no purpose, who killed for no good reason, who carried away more than they could eat, more than they could ever use in an entire lifetime. When the hordes came, the scribes would sit in silence and stillness, drawing attention away from the runners. The runners used their cunning to lead the hordes away from their pastures, away from the mountains and away from the stone village.

"Long ago, twin sisters were born in the stone village. They grew up inseparable - eating together, studying together, sitting together and coming of age together but, during the ceremony to mark their coming of age, they separated. One twin, like her father, preferred the silence and stillness of the stone. She liked to listen and to learn, to illustrate and to write and wanted nothing more than to fulfil her purpose in the stone village.

"The other twin was more like her mother and could barely contain her excitement when the day came that she could leave the stone village and run with her mother.

"By then, the stone village had already existed in the mountains for hundreds of years, and its library was immense. Over these years, the scribes had learned much more from the stone than just silence and stillness. They had learned how to move rock, how to open fissures, how to cause rock-falls, tremors and quakes, because the threat from the hordes had grown, and knowledge of a secret citadel, hidden in the mountains and filled with treasure, had leaked out into the world. The scribes could no longer be sure that the runners alone could protect them.

"The runners had come to love the chase and, although they still brought the herds to the stone village for the winter, they preferred to live permanently outside its walls. They didn't tell the scribes that they had learned how to kill. The hordes had become too many and the runners feared that the stillness of the scribes could no longer protect them, and their own cunning and resilience would soon be overwhelmed. One day, they lured a horde into a mountain trap and killed them with arrows and rocks. At first, they were ashamed of the pleasure they felt for the killing but quite soon they experienced a desire for more.

"The sisters grew old and each became the leader of her type but, by now, the scribes and runners had little understanding of each other. The scribes still felt called to sit in stillness but no longer knew why. The runners still loved to run, but now took so much pleasure in killing those whose greed exceeded their need that they forgot the real purpose of the run. The hordes were now so many that the runners were overwhelmed. The hordes were able to take to the mountains, in search of the apocryphal citadel filled with treasure. The scribes kept them at bay with earthquakes and rock-falls until there was nothing left to fall but the village itself. Before destroying the village, they took all the books to the shores of their sacred lake and sacrificed the library and themselves to their fires."

I dropped to my knees, overwhelmed by Marisa's story, overwhelmed by the effect of the truth on my being. Marisa joined me, close enough to touch, bended knee to bended knee. She reached forward to take my hands.

"Sister," she said, "look what's become of us!"

I wrapped my arms around her, nuzzled my nose into her neck, soaked her shoulder with my tears as she soaked mine. "Two ends of the same stick," I said, "but we lost sight of the stick. I destroyed everything, all human history and knowledge, hoping I could bring it back in better times."

"But you cannot bring back what matters most. You cannot bring back the memory of a time before envy, a time before greed, a time before violence. Nobody believes that anymore. I love you Kali."

"If you loved me why did you try to kill me?"

"I didn't want to kill you Kali; if I had you would be dead and Dorje would be mine. I did what I had to do. I wounded you so deeply, so invisibly that nobody could heal you, so you would have to come back to the monastery and complete the sacrifice."

Truth

The days before her lover arrived were a tangle of anticipation and anxiety. He never said he would come, never called her between visits, and yet she always knew he was on his way. He would always arrive late, after she was in bed, after she was already asleep. He would never ring the bell from the street but would wake her with his persistent tapping on her door.

She never knew how he would be - as she remembered, or with something else missing, from his mind or from his body. As usual, she tired of her other lovers, tired of her friends, wanted to be left alone, preparing for days for his knock.

She sat quietly, watching the world pass by on the street below her window. She never knew how to prepare. She would start, then change her mind. She thought to wax her legs. She took the kit from its place beneath the bathroom sink, plugged it in, watched the wax melt, watched the hairs float to the surface. Before she filtered the wax, she changed her mind and unplugged the heater. She dipped her fingers into the wax and watched it harden. She rolled the false skin into a ball and dropped it back into the liquid. He wouldn't mind that her legs weren't smooth; he probably didn't notice anyway.

As the wax hardened, she filed her nails. Of this she was sure, her lover liked to have her nails dig deep into the muscle of his back. She liked to put her nails in his flesh, liked the feeling that she could hold him forever. She filed her nails so she could dig but not draw blood; he had already given enough of his blood. She didn't want to take any more. Sometimes, when he arrived, he looked almost empty, almost drained of life. She wished she knew how to fill him again, how to transfuse some of herself into him.

During these waiting days she lost interest in food. Perhaps she wanted to weaken her body, to know something of the way his body must feel. By the time the wax had hardened it was late afternoon. The thin autumn light made her room glow as the rays cut through the dust and smoke.

She knew her lover was near, perhaps already in the country. She shuddered, realised that her fear was now stronger than her longing. She remembered their first meeting.

She was young and running. He was resting from running. They met on a tired old ferry groaning its way from Paros to Piraeus. They met on the stern rail, both gazing back to the island, both still saying goodbye, neither ready to look forward. Before she knew his name, he told her he needed her, needed her to help him through the night, maybe would need her still tomorrow when the boat arrived.

No reason came to say no and she followed him down to his cabin which smelled of burnt diesel. In the darkness of the room he asked her to take off her clothes and put her body next to his.

She discovered the first scar before she knew his face.

Her fingers fell into the place, as she explored the mass of his back, as she lay beside him, in the way he asked her to lie. She knew intuitively to say nothing and yet, the curiosity of her fingers drew her back again and again, to a place where something was missing. She was fascinated by the dent, by the way the skin curled up at its edges, by the shiny surface inside, thin and stretched like cellophane. She longed to know what was missing, what took this piece away from him. Time and again her fingers returned. Time and again she forced her hands away until, at last she was able to hold him the way he asked. In the comfort of her arms he fell asleep.

She lay awake and watched over him. Somehow, she held this massive man, made it safe for him to sleep. As he slept, she felt the tremors run through his body. Many times, she heard him call out, calling a name that she didn't have the tongue to say. As the ferry droned and shuddered its way to sunrise, she learned to love him. She loved him for the way he trusted her with his body, his fear, his dreams.

As the first light entered the cabin through the tiny porthole, she eased her body a little away from his.

She moved his head away from where she held it all night against her chest. She wanted to look at his face as he slept. It made her smile to see the peace that her holding had brought to his features. She forgot that she could have been anyone. She forgot that the only reason she was here was because she didn't say no. She felt a love she had never known before. She felt like a mother, giving simply because asked, needing nothing to justify her being here. She felt her desire, present but satisfied just by his presence. She wanted to say his name but she didn't know it yet, wouldn't know it for another year. He woke as the ferry slowed to enter the harbour. She watched as the fear returned to his face.

He sat up, unsure of where he was, not knowing who she was. He said he had to leave. He thanked her for being there. His language was simple; it was not his language. She couldn't tell which language was his. He asked her just to let him go and she agreed. She wrote her number down, overruled his hesitation, forced him to take it before he left, made him put the paper in his pocket. She forgot to write her name. When he left the cabin, she waited. She wanted him to get away. She wanted him to know he didn't need to run, at least not from her.

When she returned to the deck it was empty but for the crew. She walked ashore. She felt serene and tall. Two days later she was home again, back with her familiar home and friends and work. Her past was now the past.

She felt stronger for her night with the man. She felt freed by her night of holding his body. Her fingers longed to touch the hole in his back but she was unable to call his face to mind, just his hair - long and black and bedraggled into dreadlocks by the sea and sun.

She didn't miss him, was even surprised that she didn't miss him. With a new sense of herself, she restructured her life. She no longer felt the need for a man, but learned how to choose one when she wanted a body to hold for the night.

By the time he called again he was already forgotten. His call came in the middle of the night. His request was as simple as the first and she didn't say no. She despatched the man who lay sleeping beside her. He left quietly, without argument. He already knew the way she was.

She dozed in the warm pool of the bed until, just as the sunlight broke through the trees into her room, she heard a tapping at the door. It was a slow persistent tapping. It could have been her heartbeat. She felt the resignation in the sound as if it didn't really expect an answer. She opened the door and let him into her life. She knew no way to welcome him. She showed him into her living room. His size made the room look small. She made coffee and sat across from where he sat. She was just looking. She wanted to know how he looked.

She could see the fear, but she knew he felt safe here, with her. Her fingers wanted to touch the scar, wanted to be sure that something was still missing. His hair was still long, no longer matted but still thick and course. His big face, framed by the black of his hair and divided by the thick line of his brow reminded her of a bullock. The shape of the bones was clear beneath the dense layer of his brown skin.

As she looked, she could see his features soften. The transition was clear, just as it had been on the boat when she had watched the fear return. She knew that her being here, quietly watching him was enough to make him feel safe. He could let go of the tensions that kept the world at bay. When he finished his coffee, she took his hand and led him to the bedroom.

It was only then that she noticed the missing fingers; she hadn't seen that before. Perhaps it was because his hands were so big that it wasn't obvious. She had the urge to inspect, to raise his hand and know for sure what was gone. She restrained herself, waiting until she had undressed him, waiting until she had laid him down onto the crumple of her sheets, waiting until she had removed her clothes and put her body next to his. Now she could see, as he lay there, brown skinned and massive in the morning light, his little finger was gone. The scar extended down into a hand which ended abruptly, incomplete, in a ribbon of shiny pinks and purples knotted together along the edge. The next finger was only half a finger, ending in a twist like a sausage skin - tied off, sealing the entrance to his body. She interlaced her fingers with his. She liked the feeling of incompleteness where her little finger rested in space, alone and unheld.

Suddenly she was filled with questions, hungry for answers, for details. When she looked at his face, now passive and innocent, gazing up at the ceiling with eyes so rich and brown in the yellow light, she knew this was not the time. She knew that she would have to know, but not yet.

Now was the time to gather his face and press it to her chest. As she did so, her fingers stumbled upon another aberration. They found a ridge, hidden beneath the mat of his hair. It was a solid ridge which her fingers followed into a circle. There was no hair, just shiny skin and the ridge. Her fingers wouldn't keep off it, wouldn't stop their journey round the ridge.

Without lifting his head, without moving his eyes, he told her it was titanium. A piece of titanium had been carved and shaped and rounded and bonded to the bone, covering the place where bone was missing. A piece of his thigh, a hairless piece had been cut free and shaped and stitched to cover the metal dome. He told her how, along with the bone, he had lost a piece of his brain. More had been taken by the surgeons. He said it took a year before he knew what he lost with that piece of brain. Even now, he still discovered new things lost, names displaced, memories mislaid, words that no longer knew where they belonged.

She wanted to look inside, wanted it to be glass and not metal that kept her out.

As he spoke, he fell asleep. She remained awake, holding his face to her chest, sure that in his sleep he knew she was watching over him. He woke again as the sun was going down, woke to the bedroom bathed in shades of reds, woke to the woman watching his sleep. This time his face retained its calmness.

She said she'd be back, returned to the bed with coffee and toast and cigarettes. He wanted to talk. He wanted to talk of his wounds. He knew she would listen with the same care as she watched. He told her of his childhood, of the family whose home was taken by fire and crushed by bulldozers into the earth. He told of his people whose land had been stolen. He told of the strangeness of walking on a land where his family had walked for hundreds of years, a land which was no longer his. He told of the guns and soldiers, of the curfews and beatings. He told of the daily violence which became a war, of losing his family and losing his friends, of the people cut from his life while his eyes were closed.

He told of the night spent in a hole in the ground while the world exploded and burned around him. He told of the man who slipped into the crater beside him, the man who said he came from America. He told her how, in the midst of the inferno, the American talked about truth, talked about photographing the truth, believed that the world could be changed by the truth, that truth would stop the violence.

The American gave him a camera, a pocket full of films, a telephone number in New York. As the war raged on above them, he learned about light and frame and distance. He learned how to translate what he saw into numbers so that the camera could see what he saw. He learned how to use the camera with his eyes closed, or held with his hands behind his back, how to see what the camera could see without having to look through the lens. He learned how to capture the truth.

As the sunrise exposed the vulgarity of the night, the guns and rockets fell into a shameful silence. He took his first picture, of his mentor, the American caked in dust and blood who helped him keep his soul. His second picture recorded the moment his mentor was ripped apart as he ran into the sights of a sniper who had no soul.

He fled the country by foot, running and recording, gathering the truth until his films were full. When he finally called the number in New York he spoke to the American's wife, entrusted her with the memory of that pure and gentle man and, later, his photographs which she promised to show to the world.

And so, began a life recording other people's wars, other people's tragedies and losses.

He had nothing left to lose but himself and he lost himself piece by piece. He showed her his wounds, told her their stories, told the story of the truths he collected in return for those sacrifices. He let her touch the scars and dents she hadn't yet discovered. There was no pride in his stories. He didn't need her sympathy nor appreciation. He only needed her to listen, to watch when he returned, to let him go when it was time.

Over the years, he brought back less and less of himself to her. Piece by piece she saw him cut away, perhaps by a bullet or by a white hot metal fragment like the one that divided his leg at the knee. Sometimes, simply by what he had to see. She told little of this to her friends. All they knew was that when he came to her, she was entirely his. They didn't know his name so they never knew his work. They watched her grow older, childless, this, the woman they all thought would raise a family long before them.

Deep in the night, deep in her dreams, she heard the tapping, a hopeless tapping, first as a tree branch against the window of the cottage where her dream had taken her, and then as the feeble call from her lover at her door.

She awoke filled with fear, didn't want to answer, didn't want to be there. She searched for her courage, slowly moved towards the door, found just enough courage to open it, to let the grey and lifeless man in, to help him to the bed. He was asleep before she finished laying him down. He slept on as she rolled him back and forth, peeling away his clothes, washing him down with a warm flannel, inspecting his body for new wounds, renewing contact with old wounds.

There was nothing new to alarm her, his body was as complete as it was when last she saw him, and yet he was emptier than ever before. He slept for four days. And for four days she watched over him, sometimes raising him to the edge of his coma to pour warm soup or honey water down his throat, sometimes rolling him to change the towel filled with brown urine that leaked uncontrolled from his body.

On the fourth day he woke a little, just enough to tell her he was leaving, just enough to tell her he had lost his soul. In a whisper, fainter than the breeze outside, he told her how he killed a man, how he smashed his camera into the head of a soldier he found raping a young girl, how he rolled him off and held him as the girl fled into the woods. He told her how, as he held the dying man, he watched him briefly return.

He saw that who he held was just a boy - a boy suddenly aware that he had killed, suddenly aware that he had raped, racked with despair at what he had become, filled with fear that it would end here, alone, despised by the stranger who watched over him. He told her how, as he watched the life seeping from the boy, he realised there was no truth.

What he thought was truth, captured by his camera, was nothing more than his way to hide from that which lurked within him.

Now he saw how he used his pictures to make himself neutral, as if it were possible to be free of being human. Now he saw how, given the right moment, given the right conditions, he too could kill. He decided, in knowing that, he could no longer live. He left his soul with that boy, unable to let him go alone, brought his body back to her to say goodbye.

He closed his eyes. She held his face to her chest. She felt the warmth recede, the tension subside, his weight drop into the bed. She smelt the acetone of his last breath. She no longer needed to watch over him and fell asleep beside his empty body.

The kiss

She came to see him in his office one afternoon in September. She had booked the appointment a month before. From that first brief conversation on the phone he knew she was trouble. He had been anticipating this meeting since then. He knew nothing about her, just her voice. He wondered how, in knowing nothing but a voice, he could have so clearly predicted that first meeting.

Life with his fiancée faded. Now he never talked of marriage. When he watched her coming from the bathroom, he still knew she was beautiful but he felt no desire. He often woke at night to find his body had moved away from her, to the edge of the bed. He could no longer bear her touch. It made him feel uneasy, penetrated too much to his truth, made him want to leave his skin and flee. He started sleeping on the floor in the living room, told her it was nothing, nothing to do with her. He told her it was a difficult point in his therapy - old pain, feelings of abandonment, rage at his mother. He knew the words that satisfied his fiancée.

She wanted to help him. She wanted to support him. He knew the pleasure this gave her. He knew how much she revelled in hearing the painful history of others.

He knew how the mess of another's past helped her maintain the illusion of her own. She left him alone as he asked.

He wanted to tell her to leave, to fuck off out of his life. He wanted to tell her what to do with her empathy, her understanding, her neutral dialogue, always digging deeper into him. He didn't want her understanding. He didn't want her therapist's search for truth. He wouldn't tell her the truth. He wouldn't tell her how she bored him, how she evoked no passion, no desire in his body. He wouldn't tell her how he felt more desire for the woman whose voice he had heard only once on the phone.

She arrived on time. It was early evening, his last appointment of the day. He'd made sure of that. He'd also kept his evening free - just in case. She came into his office and sat down where he indicated, in the chair beside the window. The late summer light brought a warm reddish glow. She was as he'd imagined, her tall slim body moved with an artificial grace effected to hide a deeper uncertainty within. Her beautiful face gave away little beyond the seduction of her smile.

The firmness of her gaze suggested a challenge, daring him to contradict what she was about to tell. Her clothes were expensive, betrayed someone else's taste. He asked her why she'd come and she told him it was her boyfriend's idea. He suggested she tell him something of her life.

She told him of her childhood, of a mother who abandoned her, unable to have an abortion, unable to keep an illegitimate child because of her religion. She told of the many women who'd raised her, the aunties and grandmothers and the barren stepmother who loathed her. She told of the loneliness of life in boarding school and how she finally fled, leaving her home, her family, her country to run to London with a boyfriend.

He felt a longing in his heart, a longing to help her, to make her feel wanted. He knew the danger in what he felt. He knew that this seduction, so soon, so strong, could bring nothing but disaster. He knew that therapy would be impossible. He knew he couldn't take her on as a patient. An inner voice was screaming to get her out of his office and out of his life. By now the light had faded. They were sitting together in the half-light of his office. They were both silent, gazing at each other, relaxed, their breathing deep and synchronised, like lovers.

He heard himself tell her that she didn't need therapy, that she was doing fine, that she'd survived difficult times and had a strong will, that she could do as she wished in life. He heard himself say that he had his doubts about therapy anyway, that it was really little more than a middle class hobby, that the money would be better spent on a good holiday. He watched her laugh and wanted to take her then and there, to rip her clothes off and make love to her on the floor of his office, to fill this sacred temenos with his passion.

He heard himself tell her she didn't need to pay, that he'd be happy to meet with her and talk again, perhaps over a glass of wine. He walked her to the street and kissed her on the cheeks she coyly offered to his lips. He could smell her perfume and the deeper scent of her body. He could feel the force of her seduction as she leant towards him and he could feel the way his body wanted to reach out and draw her to him. He could feel the force of his own seduction sneaked into that innocuous, "See you again?".

They turned in opposite directions and parted. He walked around the corner to the café, sat at the bar and ordered a glass of red wine. From the attentive gaze of the waitress he knew that already, everything was different; but for a few details he was a free man.

He went home, lit a fire, sat in his bed on the living room floor staring at the flames. Some hours later his fiancée returned home. She came in timidly, quietly, checking if he wanted to talk or be left alone. He hated the way he'd broken her spirit, the way she cowered like a beaten puppy in his presence. He provoked an argument and quickly elevated it into a shouting match. In the heat of the fight he told her he couldn't bear her, couldn't stand the way she was always trying to sort him out, that he wanted to live with a lover not a therapist.

As she broke down and sobbed her huge noisy sobs, he told her that he wanted her out of his home and out of his life as soon as possible. He knew he was destroying her, destroying her life and he knew he had to act fast before his remorse got the better of him and made him care for her again.

He threw some clothes into a bag and left the apartment with his defeated fiancée wailing on the floor. Once on the street, he called an old lover and inveigled his way into her bed for the night. He lost himself in the familiarity of her body and their love-making by numbers and soon fell asleep, freed from anxiety and guilt.

The following day, he organised a more permanent place for himself to stay and called his home number. He knew his fiancée would be out and he left a short message on the answer-machine, telling her that he'd stay away for four weeks and he wanted her out of the flat by the time he returned. He said there was no going back. He was sorry for the hurt he'd caused her. He realised that he was not suited to so much intimacy. He said he just wanted time alone to work on his issues. She'd be better off without him. How right he was, she was married within the year and he never saw her again.

The following Tuesday he went to see his therapist, told him how he'd left his fiancée. He got the reaction he expected, familiar interpretations around abandonment and commitment.

He started a fight with his therapist, accused him of not being there for him, of always changing allegiances. He said he needed a therapist he could trust to work with such deep issues. He said he felt betrayed, he wouldn't continue, he would find another therapist to work with. He would pay for the two sessions notice he'd agreed to but he wouldn't come. He didn't mention the woman.

She called exactly one month after her first visit. He had left the same appointment time open and the call came straight through to his office. She invited him for dinner and he accepted. He wrote down her address. It was unnervingly close to his own. As soon as he put down the phone, he had the same sense of foreboding he'd felt when he'd first booked her appointment two months before. He left his practice and walked down into Soho, stopped at a café and bought a coffee before finding a seat out on the pavement.

The evening was fine and warm and the streets full of people - lovers arm in arm, sharing their intimacy with the world - media executives weaving their urgent way through the dawdlers. He walked around the corner to buy some wine and hailed a taxi, heading west. He arrived at her address, a large sprawling Victorian mansion block. She buzzed him in and he was waved on by the concierge, one of those people whose gaze seemed to imply guilt. He walked up the grand carpeted stairs to her apartment on the second floor.

The door was open and he let himself in and called her name. She returned his call from somewhere far away and he set off down a long wide corridor to find her sitting in front of the television in the living room. The apartment was enormous and he passed four doors before he found her. Another corridor stretched into the distance beyond where she sat. The place was elegant but uncared for, clothes abandoned on the floor or draped messily on every radiator. He passed the kitchen before he reached her, a clutter of unwashed plates, spills and bin-liners full of rubbish.

She turned and smiled that beautiful naive smile just at the point where he knew he shouldn't be there. Too late, he couldn't resist, he kissed her on the cheeks and sat down beside her on the sofa.

She was casually dressed, t-shirt, leggings, bare feet. She behaved as if she hadn't expected him to come. He offered the wine and she went to the kitchen and rummaged, returned with two clean glasses and a cork-screw. She told him she hadn't had time to cook, but she would send out for pizza. She asked him if he liked to smoke grass. He hadn't smoked for years but he didn't refuse. She expertly rolled a small joint of pure grass, took a long drag and passed it to him. It tasted good, very fresh, but after a couple of drags, he regretted his decision; smoking weed helped him see too clearly. He watched as she crossed the room to put on some music and saw a child hiding in the mannerisms of a woman.

When she saw he was watching, she smiled, a satisfied smile and, again he felt that sense of foreboding. She returned to the sofa, sat close to him, snuggling her body next to his. He felt the friction of desire and misgivings but he put his arm around her shoulder and drew her closer. When he gave in to her it felt good. Mellowed by the smoke, with her body next to his, with her smell in his nostrils, his seriousness left him. He let himself go.

The pizza arrived and they hardly touched it. She put on a movie. They smoked a little more, drank some wine, slowly sank down into the sofa until he lay folded along her back, his arms wrapped round her body, her fingers entwined with his fingers and his nose nuzzled in the dark aroma at the back of her neck. They fell asleep.

As the night deepened and darkened, as he drifted through different layers of sleep, as the birds started singing and the morning light crept into the room, as the traffic increased on the streets, as he felt her body dreaming next to his, she became familiar to him, as if he had known her forever. They drank coffee and ate pastries downstairs from her apartment and then walked hand in hand through Holland Park to Portobello market.

He wanted to ask her so many questions but he knew he had to wait. He already knew she was a master of disguise.

He bought an antique mirror for her bathroom and some fruit from the stalls. They had lunch on the street outside a small Italian restaurant. He couldn't keep his eyes from her face, from those big soft seductive eyes and the lips that he hadn't yet dared to kiss. Her expression changed endlessly between that irresistible childish innocence, animal cunning and shame. Again, he became aware of his inner conflict, of his wish to thank her for the evening and leave and his wish to give himself completely to the trap which was now drawing him in.

She said she had to go, she had a date with a friend, could she see him tomorrow? Would he come in the afternoon? After she left, he sat and drank another coffee and smoked. He missed her already. He paid and left, walked back through the market and across the park to his apartment. He managed to get in without meeting his neighbours. She was gone. His home was dull and flat. She had taken all her paintings and pretty fabrics. The vases were empty of flowers. The place was colourless, lifeless, with an atmosphere of death.

He felt his grief begin to choke him. He kept it at bay by cleaning and tidying and rearranging. He wanted to chase out his fiancée's presence as fast as he could. He opened all the windows and lit incense in every room. He rearranged the bedroom and changed the linen. He took out old paintings from behind the wardrobe to cover the emptiness of the walls. He went out to the supermarket to buy supplies to stock the kitchen and then to the florist where he bought bunches of flowers to fill every vase.

As evening closed in he had reclaimed his space. He lit a fire, opened some wine and, at last sat down to rest. He longed for his fiancée and he longed for his new lover. Where was she now? He felt uneasy. He called her number but got the answer-machine. He didn't leave a message. He drank enough wine to crush his conscience and make him weary. He fell into a dream riddled sleep in front of the fire.

He woke early, the sun just edging its light through the trees into his room. His first thought was to call his lover but he knew he mustn't. He made coffee and toast and returned to his bed. He wanted his lover to be here, to share this beautiful morning with him. He had to wait. He wanted to sleep away the time but sleep had fled. He imagined her, pictured her pretty face and her long, slim body. Today he knew he would take her. Today he would give himself to her. His fantasy pleased him, left no room for the memories of his fiancée.

It was hard to imagine how much his life had changed in the last month. He was happy with himself. He was happy with his intuition. He was happy with his spontaneity. He was happy with his callous honesty and the way he'd pruned from his life the people who no longer gave him what he wanted. He was in control of his life, taking what was offered, without concern for getting it right.

He was free, forging his own destiny. In this fog of inflation, he subdued all the dissenting voices of his inner world. He felt power and loved it.

The afternoon came soon enough and he walked to his lover's home. On the way he bought flowers and fruit from the Persian shop, flat bread imported from Canada, butter and quince jelly. When he arrived at his lover's door it was open as before and he found her lying in her large crumpled bed. She was naked under a single sheet.

He left the provisions in the kitchen, arranged the flowers in a vase and returned with them to her room. He took off his clothes and climbed into bed beside her. It was easy to undress with her; it felt completely natural. He cuddled in beside her and at last took the opportunity to kiss her lovely mouth. She responded immediately. His desire for her mounted and he straddled her and stroked the slim athletic form of her body. As his hands moved down her belly to the edge of her pubis, she grasped his wrists tightly, restraining any further movement.

"No!"

He was terrible with rejection, felt embarrassed and ashamed, looked away from her, wanted to bury his face in the pillows. He apologised, asked what was wrong. She turned away from him, bit into her lower lip, tears welling up in her eyes.

She turned back and gave him one of her disarming smiles. He wanted to know what was wrong, begged her to tell him. He felt heavy. He already knew that what she would tell him would be unmanageable but he pretended it would be alright. He told her that he could take it, that he wanted to know all of her, no secrets.

She told him how, when she first came to London, she had lived with her boy-friend from back home, but he abandoned her. She was living in a hostel in Camden. She met a girl at a club who introduced her to her madam. The money was good. Sometimes she worked for rich men, men who could afford to take girls like her across the world in private jets just to have them there, like trophies. There were businessmen, men with wives and children who wanted to take her shopping, to dress her in the clothes they chose, to take her to the theatre or the latest restaurant or on a trip to Paris or Rome or New York. They paid her to do all the things they loathed doing with their wives. She had to pretend she loved them, pretend she was their lover, ignore the bundles of money they stuffed into her bag. She would go to business lunches and functions and meet other rich men with young girls. These were men for whom the grand house, the fast car, the wife and children meant nothing, compared to the power to pay a young woman to pretend they were interesting. She was hired by men who wanted a beautiful, well-bred, intellectual.

Other men wanted women who looked like tramps or women who looked like boys.

She told her story to him in a torrent, an unstoppable confession. He was fascinated by this world of which he knew nothing. He'd never thought that prostitution was such a business, so well organised and normal. He'd only been aware of the street walkers and kerb crawlers of King's Cross or the picture cards stuck up in telephone boxes.

She told him how, for the last six months, she'd had only one client. She didn't see him so often. He wanted to help her. Sometimes he treated her like a daughter, encouraged her to study, paid her rent and gave her an allowance. Sometimes he treated her like his lover, pretended he would leave his wife and live with her. Sometimes he treated her like a whore and she didn't know how to say no, she was scared he would just stop paying. She had never saved any money. She squandered it, ashamed of how it came to her.

Last night he took her for dinner and to the theatre. He brought her home. He wanted her body. She told him she was tired. She could see he was sad. She could see he needed her. She gave him her body. She didn't let him take her on the bed. She told him she wanted it on the floor, in the sitting room. She wanted to keep him out of her bed. She was sorry.

He didn't know what to say; he was out of his depth. He said he would make some tea and toast and left the room. In the living room he saw her clothes strewn on the floor where they had been ripped from her body. On the table there was a pile of cash, fifty pound notes, carelessly thrown down.

He made the tea and toast which he buttered and spread with quince jelly. When he returned to the bedroom she was sitting with her head on her knees and weeping.

He set down the tray and took her in his arms. She told him she knew he would leave her now. He wanted to say yes, he had to, he couldn't cope with this. But he said no, that he loved her, that he would help her. He knew the words he said had been said to her by many men before. She gave herself to his arms, as his lover, an expert, too practiced in the art of pleasuring men. He could think only of all the other men who'd been with her before him and he wondered what she thought, if she thought of him. Then he knew she wasn't thinking at all, she'd left her body to him and hidden herself away until it was safe to return.

When she did return, she turned to him and smiled, kissed his face and told him she loved him. He believed her because he was already in love with her. She said she would make it alright, that she would get rid of the man, that she would find a way.

He said he would help; he would do everything he could. He knew it was true and he wished it were not.

Over the following weeks they spent more and more time together. Their love-making became more natural. Sometimes she stayed with her body, sometimes she couldn't respond, could only cry, just wanted to be held by him.

He neglected his work, neglected his patients. In one week alone more than half of them asked to end their treatment. He thought perhaps his fiancée had put the word out about him, but he knew it wasn't that. He pretended he didn't care, refused to take on new patients, behaved as if his practice was full.

He cleared a week in his diary and arranged a trip to Paris with his lover. By now he was staying with her most of the time. They had tidied her place and, he supposed, as long as he was here nobody else would be. The day before they were due to leave, she was silent, unavailable. He asked her what was wrong. She told him the man wanted her for the night. He was in London, staying at Claridge's, wanted her there. She didn't know how to refuse. If she said no, she was sure he would stop paying her rent and she would be homeless.

He didn't know how to say no. He could offer no alternative. He couldn't pay her rent. He couldn't put large sums of cash on the table. She said it didn't happen very often, she would find a way to end it, but tonight she had to go, perhaps tonight she could tell him it was over.

In silence he watched as she got ready to leave. She dressed and made up. She never dressed and made-up like this for him. He wasn't sure if it pleased him or not. He told himself it was her disguise so that the man didn't get the real her. He asked if she kissed him.

"No, never, he disgusts me."

She left and he spent the night in her bed watching movies. She returned at five in the morning, threw off her clothes and climbed into bed beside him. She had a small bruise on her neck. He couldn't touch her. They lay side by side on the bed until it was time to leave. The taxi came and took them to the airport. They were mostly silent until they got to Paris.

They stayed in a friend's apartment in Belleville. She was away and had left the key with the concierge. They could use her room. He loved that room with its big windows opening out onto a yard full of flowers. He took his lover into the room and undressed her, and laid her down on the bed. She was passive. He remembered that this was her second invasion in twelve hours but he continued. He wanted to fuck her. He wanted to make her cry. He wanted her to beg his forgiveness, to promise never to hurt him again. She was silent and, in her silence, tears flowed down the sides of her face into the pillow.

He felt like a client, given into, victorious, possessing her because he could. He told himself that at least he wasn't paying. But he knew he was, he was paying dearly, he was paying with his soul. Her soul didn't return for several days. They spent too much time in awkward silences, in the streets, in the markets, in the churches, in the galleries, without enthusiasm for all the places he wanted to share with her. On the third day she told him she was pregnant. He wanted to be sure it was his. Of course it was his, she always used condoms with her clients. Of course she did, she told him so and he knew it was true - anything to keep some distance. He told her they should keep it; he would make it possible. He was lying. His life was in tatters. Since meeting her he couldn't work, had nothing left to give, no wish to give to anyone but her.

When they returned to London, he moved in with her. He planned to rent his own flat to a friend. She told her client she had a boyfriend. She told him she couldn't be his lover anymore. He stopped paying the rent, stopped leaving large sums of money on the table.

Somehow, for a while, she managed to find rolls of money hidden in boots or pockets or forgotten bags. Somehow with that, with the little he made from his patients and the expectation of rent it looked like they might get by. But soon he was spending on credit, buying her presents because she always looked like she needed a present. One night, as they lay together in the bath, she told him she would go to New York.

She had clients there who wanted her. In just one week she could make twenty thousand dollars. That would keep them for a while, until they got their lives together. He had no response. He didn't know if he was hurt or furious or proud. He was stuck in a long silent pause. He stared at her, searched his mind for something to say. There was nothing.

Finally, he just said no, climbed out of the bath, lay his drenched and wretched body down on the bed and begged for sleep to take him away. He didn't know if she came to him that night, but when he woke up the next day she was gone. She returned two days later to find him still lying in the bed. She told him she'd had an abortion. She told him she was going to New York, to stay with a friend, to recover. She wouldn't work while she was there. He had nothing to fear. She loved him. He was still silent as she packed her bag and left.

The Friday after she left, he was sitting on his bed. In front of him were pages from his local free paper, pages full of personal services, massage services and escorts. He called a few and found himself discussing prices with professional brokers. There was a small lineage ad amongst all the other displays. It said simply:

'Lucy, young Spanish girl offers full body to body massage'.

He called the number and got straight through. She didn't speak very good English, but he arranged for her to come round. Half an hour later, he heard the sound of a taxi stopping downstairs. He went down and opened the door.

She was pretty and young. He invited her into his home, into his bedroom which was lit by fire-light and candles. He offered her a glass of wine and they sat on the bed, freshly made with white cotton sheets. They talked for a while and she told him that she'd come to England to improve her language. She asked for the money. She counted it and put it into her bag.

He didn't know how to begin. He didn't know how to go straight for the body. He needed relationship. He needed seduction. He also knew that it was the last thing she needed. She reminded him that his time was limited, that she had a car coming within the hour. She undressed, removing everything but her suspenders and stockings. He supposed that men must like that. He didn't. He asked her to take them off. She helped him out of his clothes and caressed his body.

Her touch was sensitive and attentive. He was surprised, perhaps even shocked. He had wanted something more professional, more distant than this. She was beautiful naked. He inspected her body for marks but found none.

She lay down beside him and he looked into her eyes. He desired her. He wanted to kiss her but knew this would not be allowed. His lover told him that kissing was infinitely more intimate than fucking.

Lucy broke away from his gaze and nuzzled her way down his body. When she reached his sex, she produced a condom and deftly rolled it on. She took a tissue from the box beside the bed and wiped it clean before taking him in her mouth. Again, he was surprised, he hadn't expected this but he was reassured by her expertise, by her well-practiced technique, reassured that this was her job and not her vocation. She asked if he wanted to make love. He said yes.

He wanted to say no. He wanted to say no, I want you to stay with me and talk with me like a friend until the morning. He supposed this was usual, that the client often had the fantasy that this was his lover and not simply a hired body. She helped him enter her body. She was moist and hot. He had wanted her to be unprepared and unwilling. He had wanted her to be dry and in need of the tubes of lubrication he had seen in the drawer beside his lover's bed. He hadn't wanted any sign that she might enjoy this.

They made love. He was slow, unsure that he could come but he wanted to complete the process, to experience it all, to reassure himself. As he moved, he felt her body heat and soften. He felt her grip on his back tighten as she drew him closer to her, deeper into her body. Her breathing changed, her breaths becoming shorter and more urgent. Her movements became free and uncontrolled. As her body lurched into a spontaneous orgasm, she gripped his head and pulled his mouth to her mouth, pressed her kiss deep into his lips, sucked the air from his lungs, exhaled the fire from her belly into his face.

He lay gazing at her. Her eyes were closed. There was sweat on her forehead. Her hot body relaxed beneath him. Her breathing was quiet, almost as if she were asleep. When she opened her eyes, she looked embarrassed, shocked. She said she had to go; her car was waiting. He let go of her and she dressed without looking at him again. She was flustered, urgent. She said she would let herself out. And then she was gone. He lay on the bed, in that pool of damp heat and wept.

Tantra

Her body looked compressed as if it had never fully unwound from the plump container of babyhood. What was lacking in torso length seemed to stem from a shortage of spine, as if one or two vertebrae had failed to take their proper place and, instead added their mass to her pelvis. It was always her pelvis that arrived first, projecting itself forward, her legs obliged to follow in its wake. It was her pelvis that spoke first, long before her clever and carefully strung words found form. Her words were no more than a superficial surface on a seduction already done. No man ever really heard the words - they were just time passed between the first attraction and the final completion of her pelvis.

Her pelvis found its place between his legs where he sat at the bar stool. It had a heat so intense that the noise of the band and the clamour at the bar receded. He gazed down at her, at this small woman who had followed her pelvis to the place where it lodged itself between his thighs. She gazed up with the face of a child, her boyish face framed with a pampered woman's hairstyle, her long neck accented with huge beads of Tibetan amber and sky-dancer amulets. Her eyes sparkled and when he offered a drink they laughed.

"A drink? I don't think so."

Her French accent was the perfect French accent, conveying as it did that subtle blend of playfulness and admonishment. Together they both looked down. Together they both acknowledged what he had, until now, pretended not to notice. As if she needed a drink!

They were both still laughing as they took the taxi south across the river to her house. She always brought her own music with her and as always, the driver obliged by playing it loud and denying himself the pleasure of hearing the sounds she made.

He didn't see too much of the Georgian decor she had described during the journey, just the dark wood panelled hallway with its elephant leg umbrella stand and the sinister ancestral oil paintings that lined the stairway and corridor that led to her room. She quietly closed the door behind her.

"Sshhh, I don't want my husband to wake up."

Before he had time to run, she added, "He's working early tomorrow and hates to be woken up."

It was enough to calm his panic. As he turned back from the door, she was already naked on the enormous wrought iron bed that dominated the room. He stared transfixed as she arranged her crystals and stones in a large circle around where she sat amongst the French linen and embroidered bolsters.

Her eyes led his eyes down to her substantial and craving pelvis just as her fingers withdrew a large quartz wand from that place between her legs. She raised it to her waiting tongue and with that now familiar sparkle in her eyes called him to her.

"Your turn now."

As instructed, he shed his clothes and sat cross-legged in the circle of stones and crystals. With great agility she clasped her arms around his neck and lowered her pelvis onto him. She drew him deep inside her with the seething peristalsis of her vagina.

He reached his limit, but she continued to draw in his flesh, one hand still clinging to his shoulder, the other sliding the quartz wand between his perineum and the horse hair mattress. The intensity of physical sensation was marred by fearful feelings at the force with which she held him. She clasped his head with both hands and forced him to look into her eyes, refused to let him escape into disassociation. Her eyes no longer sparkled with the child-like playfulness he had seen before. They were deep and archaic eyes that dismissed his fear, not with reassurance, but with the certainty and inevitability they conveyed. As she held him with her grip and gaze, he felt her contractions recommence, felt the skin across his belly and thighs tighten and stretch, felt his inner tubes and ligaments stretch and submit, felt his own contractions where her crystal wand pressed against his perineum, felt his life-force succumb and pour unstaunched into her pelvis.

Still she held his head. Still she held his gaze. Still she refused to let his body collapse even as she emptied it of its fluids, draining the liquids from every ruptured tubule and cell. Still she insisted on his attention with her eyes, eyes that gained depth and force with each contraction until at last, she had drained him to the core and threw the husk of his body down against the sheets.

Next door her husband stirred, colour and breath returning, fluids flowing, his emaciated body coming back to life.

Nine airports

I   Rome FCO

The plane plunged through the bright early morning light and juddered to a halt on the rough tarmac of Fiumicino airport. She stepped out into the sunshine and down the stairs, took deep breaths of Italian air, filled with a sense of freedom after the long cramped flight from New York. Her body trembled slightly in anticipation of the unknown.

She lingered by the aircraft wing as long as she could to avoid waiting on the overcrowded airport bus. She realised that part of her excitement was from leaving behind her complicated and unsatisfying New York life. She knew that from this moment on everything would be different. She found it hard to call to mind the lover she had abandoned to his melancholic city life. She knew she would never be with him again. She allowed herself to be coerced onto the bus and taken to the airport building. For her there was no rush, she had twelve hours to wait for her onward flight. She soon realised that airports are no place for the patient and found herself jostling for a place at the baggage carousel that, even now, stood still.

She found herself standing next to a woman she recognised from the plane. She'd wanted to speak with her when she first saw her in the airport lounge at JFK. She'd been attracted by her elegance and by the long line of her neck. She'd been drawn to her serenity, by the aura of quietness she threw around herself.

The opportunity to talk hadn't come before; the woman boarded the plane with first class passengers and was separated from her throughout the flight. At last they could speak. She told the woman that she was returning to her homeland, for the first time since her parents fled when she was just six years old. She told of her excitement of seeing the family she barely remembered, of rediscovering her grandparents and aunts and uncles. She told of the thrill of finally being in Europe for the first time, if only for twelve hours, that she felt this was where she really belonged.

The woman said she was returning to live in Rome although she originally came from Umbria. She'd left her country home to become a dancer. She'd been 'discovered' by the brother of a famous film director and started acting. Her acting took her to Los Angeles and now, after fifteen years, she was coming home. The woman suggested she take a short trip into Rome where she could pass the time as she waited for her onward flight. She wrote down a list of places to see and her telephone number in case she returned for longer someday.

The carousel started turning and their conversation was lost in the tension mounting around them. She felt thrilled by this meeting, felt she'd found an older sister or perhaps, a mentor. She knew she had to meet this woman again.

The woman collected her bag, kissed her on the cheeks and was gone. She collected her own bag and checked it into left luggage. She was not allowed to check in for her onward flight, it was too early. She changed some dollars and found herself rich in lira. She took a taxi to the city, to the Vatican. She didn't know why the Vatican. Perhaps she wanted to see the Sistine Chapel but she wasn't sure.

She walked in the grand square of St. Peter's. She felt lonely, a little aimless. She wasn't sure why she was here, didn't appreciate the beauty, couldn't take it in. She found a café, a seat on the pavement, a cappuccino, a croissant. She felt a longing, a deep longing from her heart. It was not for her lover; she checked, she felt nothing for him. This longing was for something she didn't yet know.

As she sat, the square filled with tourists. She no longer wanted to be here. She didn't want to see the Sistine Chapel. She didn't want all these people, all their hunger. She called for the bill and reached into her bag for her purse. It was gone, and with it her passports and air ticket. She turned out her bag, emptied it onto the pavement, searched and searched again, knowing it was futile but searching still as her eyes filled with tears.

She remembered the lira in her pocket, left some to cover the bill, gathered her things and rushed from the café, before anyone could see her distress. How could she have let this happen? She found a quiet place, a small passage, away from the busy street where she could cry. She cried until she was empty of tears. In the dryness she found her will, her determination to survive.

She took a taxi back to the airport and on the journey planned her moves. Once there, she talked to various officials, from the airline, from the airport, from the police, from the embassy. She demanded their help. They couldn't refuse. She called her brother in America. He faxed copies of her papers: her ticket, her passports, her driving licence. She called the embassy, faxed the copies, arranged a meeting with an official at the airport. She called the credit card companies and cancelled her cards.

Everything was done. She knew her options. She could get American papers that would allow her to travel in Europe. She couldn't continue her journey to her family without the passport of her homeland. She had only a little money. The airline would put her onto a flight to New York tomorrow and put her up for the night in a hotel near the airport. That was it, everything was done, fate was sending her home. She collected her bag and checked into the hotel.

She took a shower, a long, long shower, washing away her despair. She would go home, she had no choice, but already everything was different. She had found her power and she would never give it away again.

She unpacked her bag and found her wallet. She'd forgotten she'd put it there. It contained her money and her credit cards. She called the card companies and reinstated her cards. Now she was not so sure. She didn't have to return. She called the woman from the airport and asked if they could meet. They arranged to meet in a bar in Trastévere. The woman didn't have much time, she was going out for dinner.

She took a taxi to the bar and was shown to the table where the woman waited for her. They embraced and in the firmness of the hug she let go of the rigid determination that had got her through. She sat and told her story. She told of the square, the thief, the papers, the calls, the officials and the sadness she felt for not going on to see her grandparents, her aunts, her uncles, her parents in the place they belonged. The woman said something in a language that sounded familiar, like Farsi, but she couldn't understand. The woman translated from Arabic,

"Regret nothing, lest it be for the best."

The woman explained that her grandmother was from Palestine and taught her many things from her culture - not the language but many aphorisms. She also taught her how to read coffee cups.

"Perhaps you need a reading?"

She drained the expresso, turned the cup three times with her left hand and turned it over into the saucer as instructed. The woman took the cup and her gaze softened on the powdery stain of the grounds. Her body softened. Her breathing softened. She waited, calmly, for the truth to reveal itself. Finally, the woman looked up and translated. The future was open. Nothing would be the same. She should go to Barcelona. That was all. This was just a moment in time. Everything was possible. All choices were possible. The coffee cup revealed only one way, not the only way, we always had the final choice, we had to use our will. She had to leave, she was already late, they would meet again. The woman paid the bill and left.

She left soon after and went to the train station to buy a ticket to Barcelona. There were no couchettes available - only seats. It would take seventeen hours. She went to the hotel, packed her bag and checked out.

She went to the airport and confirmed that she would fly to New York on her original booking. She returned to the train station, bought sandwiches, fruit and water. She felt good.

II   Paris CDG

The previous month had been painfully aimless. He'd wanted to go away but nowhere inspired him. His life was on hold. He'd been waiting for fate to point its finger. He hated these times. He no longer trusted his fate. He no longer trusted his own intuition to wait. He used to believe he was a traveller in a benign and abundant universe, that all he had to do was ask and wait. Now he wasn't so sure. Now he feared his own passivity and was suspicious of the stories he told himself. Now he no longer knew what to ask for, how to tolerate the void he felt, how to fill a void for which he had no name.

He'd sent the final draft of a novel to his agent. Experience told him it was always like this, there was always a void, he'd emptied himself out, he had to give time to recover his sense of himself. For the moment, he believed this new story.

He called some friends in France, they were going to India and he wanted to talk before they left. They offered their house in the forest if he wanted a retreat. He wanted to see them. He was tired of his solitude. He was tired of his thoughts. He was tired of his habits. He was tired of his own smell. He needed a change and would come the next day, just for a while, just until they left. The following afternoon he packed a small bag and took a taxi to Waterloo station.

He booked a seat on the next train through the tunnel and walked over the river to the Strand. He'd forgotten there was so much life in the world. He hadn't been out for months except for the occasional walk in a park or a late beer in a bar, to remind himself he was still human.

He noticed he was rushing and remembered there was no need, there was nothing to do. He slowed down his pace, just for a moment, then found he was rushing again. He gave in to the rush. He needed time to slow down, time to find a new speed. Life in the forest would help. He drank coffee in a bar near the Strand and hurried back to the station. He loved train travel; it retained a charm that had long since deserted flying. He settled into his seat.

The motion of the train quickly rocked him to sleep; that was their beauty. He never enjoyed sleeping so much nor remembered his dreams so well. He woke briefly as the train approached the tunnel, took a deep breath as it descended beneath the channel, returned to his inner life.

He was woken again by the evening light stretching across the flatlands north of Paris. The train accelerated to full speed and he went to the bar to buy Champagne to celebrate the sense of exhilaration it brought. He finished the glass with a toast to Paris as the train reached Gare Du Nord. He had to rush across Paris to catch the last train south to the forest.

He had just enough time to call his friends and arrange for them to meet him. Once on board he began to feel some sense of relaxation; there was nothing more to do but look out for station signs in the darkness. Ten minutes out of Paris he heard someone crying behind him. For a minute he was frozen, afraid to turn to look in case he intruded.

He felt like a foreigner, self-conscious, then stupid for his reaction. He heard another tearful gasp and turned to look at the frail girl crying behind him. She looked pale and undernourished. Even her crying was weak and lifeless. He asked if he could help and found she spoke much better English than he did French. She told him she'd lived in London. She'd been working on a clothes stall in Camden market. She found God through some people she met on the street. She worked in the church mission, helping the homeless and hungry. She returned to France to try to reconcile her relationship with her family. Now she worked in Paris, in a homeless shelter, and was on her way to the family home where she lived.

Her name was Ange. She said it meant angel. He thought she looked like an angel; a distraught angel overwhelmed by the burden of her work. He wanted to sit next to her, to put an arm around her shoulders, to take the weight for a moment. He remained in his seat and she told him how she was trying to bring the word of God to her family. She told him how they argued, how she feared for her family, how they feared for her.

He told her perhaps it was better to leave her family to their own destiny, not to preach to them. He thought her family might find God through her actions and not through her words. He thought that her mission was to live as a Christian and not as an evangelist. He didn't tell her that she wasn't much of an advert for God.

He didn't know where his words came from. As the train pulled into his stop she was smiling. She said he was right. She felt inspired by his words. He waved good-bye from the platform and stepped out into the car-park and the arms of his friends. It was a warm reunion and soon they were speeding through the village to the house in the forest. It was like coming home, to his favourite home, with the silence of the trees, the company of horses, chickens and dog.

It took him two days to slow down, each day riding bareback in the forest, melting tensions from his muscles in the Jacuzzi, cooking and eating together, playing pool or cards or music late into the evening.

He slept in a huge feather bed in the conservatory and watched the stars through the tree tops. Although he felt at home he didn't feel at ease. Again, his friends invited him to stay after they left, but he knew he had to move on. He couldn't explain the discomfort he felt. Here, in the forest, he had everything he could want and was with his best friends in the world but still, he had to go. They understood.

He decided to go to Ibiza. He'd been there many times before, knew the island well, knew where to go to be private and where to go for a crowd. He knew people who spent their summers there. It was a place that gave him the choice of nature and night-life. He called an agency and booked a flight for the following day. He had one last meal with his friends in the forest. Tomorrow he would leave. In two days, they would leave for India.

In the morning they drove through the forest to Paris Charles de Gaulle. They drove into the tangle of roads that served the airport terminals. Soon they were lost on the tangle of roads. Soon they were on a road that led away from the airport with nowhere to turn. At last, they found a place to turn and tried again. Again, they were lost on the tangle. They were on a road from where they could see his terminal but none of them could see how to get there. They stopped as close as they could and he set off by foot after farewells on the kerb-side.

When he reached the terminal, his flight had boarded and the plane was leaving. He stopped, bought a café au lait and a croissant, sat at a table in the airport terminal. He watched the craziness of all the travellers around him. He drank his coffee, ate his croissant, smoked a cigarette. He felt calm, free from the craziness. He had nowhere to go. There was no hurry. He called his answer-machine in London. There was a message from a friend inviting him to a retreat at a house by the beach south of Barcelona.

There was an empty apartment waiting for him in Barcelona. There was a number for him to call for the key. He found a flight to Barcelona and booked a ticket.

III   Barcelona BCN

He arrived from the airport at Barcelona Sants railway station and made a call. He took down directions of the place he had to go. He walked out into the streets, onto the broad boulevard outside the station and then north, up a small side street towards the office where he would collect the key. He was happy to be back in this city. He could tolerate everything here, the cars on the pavement, the dog shit on the streets, the car-horns, the jostling for space. In this city, another self emerged: calmer, more patient, more open, more alive. He collected the key and was offered a lift down to the house by the beach at the weekend. He took the subway to the Ramblas and walked through the familiar streets of the gothic quarter to Passeig Del Born.

The apartment was a short walk from the Basilica de Santa Maria del Mar, an incredible Gothic church that he'd failed to visit before. The apartment was dark and cool, a series of rooms set along a crooked corridor. The shutters were closed. He found the room he liked most and left his bag. He opened the shutters in the living room, stuck his head out over the geraniums and gazed out, first towards Santa Maria del Mar, and then over the roof of the old market towards the sea. He could see into the rooms across the road. There was no sign of life.

The geraniums were dry. He watered them, watered all the plants in the apartment. He made tea, weak black tea with sugar, sat down on the sofa and dozed.

When he woke from his siesta, he took a shower and sat by the phone to call some friends. Nobody he knew was in the city. Everybody had left with the heat, to beach houses where they could cool off in the breeze from the sea. He went out into the streets. The city was empty, lifeless, given over to foolish tourists who, like him, found themselves here at the wrong time. All the interesting shops and bars were closed. The holiday had begun. The only places open were those that thrived on tourist money, cheap fast-food restaurants that saturated every city with their dull uniformity.

By the time he reached the Ramblas he felt he was being engulfed again, by that familiar feeling of being in the wrong place. The Ramblas was as he remembered it, with its magazine stalls, flower vendors and pet shops - shuttered, alas. The atmosphere was not as he remembered it. It was full of crowds of tourists interspersed with dealers and thieves. There were people selling cheap trinkets and nasty science fiction pictures spray painted with aerosols that filled the air with toxic solvents. Every twenty paces a busker stood on a box playing at statues, waiting for 100 pesetas in return for some pitiful gesture or a photo pose with a child, who had already learned to substitute a snapshot for real life.

This, the city that used to ooze sex and intrigue was now just another backdrop for a photographic record of exploited and unexperienced lives.

He turned away from it all, back into the little streets and alleys of the gothic quarter. He didn't know what to do with himself. He didn't know whether to wait in Barcelona until his friends returned or go down to the beach at the weekend. Perhaps he should return to London, go home, organise his life. He arrived at Santa Maria del Mar and went inside, found a place on a pew and sat with his head resting on the pew in front.

He was never sure what to do in church. He'd never had instruction and the rituals seemed alien. He once tried to cross himself with holy water as he'd seen others do, but it felt false. He didn't know how to pray, what to ask for, even if he was permitted to ask at all. He waited, decided just to wait, to feel the silence, the heavy silence that filled certain old churches.

He would leave tomorrow. If he didn't know what to do, better to do nothing at home where at least there was some familiarity. He went to the supermarket to buy something to eat. He would stay home, be quiet, sleep early, take a flight back to London in the morning. As he searched the shelves for something to satisfy the hunger which was not even for food, he heard a voice ask in English for matches.

He looked as a woman turned away from the counter and was gone, a woman he could hardly see but who, nevertheless, seized his attention. He gathered a few things, some cheese, tomatoes, bread, water. He paid and left. On the street he looked but there was no sign of her. He returned to the apartment and put the shopping in the kitchen. He sat for a moment; he didn't want to sit. He put on the kettle; he didn't want tea. He looked at the food; he no longer wanted to eat. Nothing appealed to him. He felt caged, trapped by indecision, by not knowing, aimless and futile. He couldn't bear to be here alone.

He left the apartment, wanted to find a bar or a restaurant. Most were closed. He crossed the square into a small street he had not been down before. It led to the sea. The street was quiet. The shutters were down. He saw a light shining out onto the pavement. As he passed by, he looked into a bar. Sitting by the door, sitting alone, was the woman he'd seen before. He turned around, walked into the bar, bought a beer, sat down beside her, not too near but near enough to talk. He asked where she was from, said he'd seen her before, heard her voice, heard she spoke English.

She told him her story, of her journey to Rome, of the thief, of the woman, of the seventeen hours sitting on a train. She told him how she'd come here because she thought she should but she couldn't see why. She told him how she'd begun to doubt her decision, how she felt uncertain, how she felt lonely, how she didn't know what to do now.

She told him how she'd gone out to eat, had eaten alone, had eaten too much, had gone back to her room to sleep. She told him she'd felt uneasy in her room on her own, how she couldn't rest, couldn't keep still, how she went to the supermarket to buy some cigarettes, came to this bar to drink and smoke.

He told her his story; it sounded like hers. He invited her to eat. She was full but would watch him. He didn't want to eat.

They went to a bar he'd passed earlier, a special place, in an abandoned and squatted cinema. It was home to a community of Catalan punks. The woman who served their beer gave them a card with directions to another place some friends were running, on the other side of the Ramblas.

They talked and drank beer. He told her he thought the thief in Rome was really an angel. They walked across the Ramblas, out into the little streets to the west, found the place on the card, found where the people of Barcelona hid in the summer months, a small bar in an old butcher's shop, with gaudy decoration and good music. Their talking came easily and their bodies soon found each other as they shared a stool at a table. Later, as they walked down the marina to the beach, he realised they were hand in hand.

If you asked either of them, they wouldn't remember how it happened, how their hands found each other.

A forgotten beach lounger was waiting for them on the edge of the tide. They lay together, watching the low waves roll in, stopping always at the same line. They didn't kiss. Despite the closeness and familiarity of their bodies they didn't kiss. It was as if their bodies were old friends but their mouths knew they were still strangers.

They decided to leave the following morning for Cadaqués. He'd been there many years before. He didn't remember it well, just that he loved it. He didn't mention that he'd longed to go there with a lover. With this moment of resolution, they left the beach and he walked her to her hotel, just around the corner from his apartment. They agreed to meet early in the morning, on the avenue outside the supermarket.

In the morning he woke early and showered and packed. He left a note for the owner of the apartment, who remained a stranger, and let himself out. There was an hour to wait before their meeting and he went for a coffee in the bar near the church of Santa Maria del Mar. He was nervous, feared she would not arrive, feared that the evening was just an illusion of drink. He went back to the avenue and sat on the bench outside the supermarket, allowed his gaze to drift along the line of trees to the church. He saw her exit the church and walk down the steps towards him. She told him how she'd felt nervous and couldn't understand what she was doing. She'd gone into the church to ask for help. Now she felt she was doing the right thing.

They took a taxi to the railway station and bought tickets for the next train to Figueras. From there they would take a bus to Cadaqués. The ease with which they started their journey set a precedent for the time that they shared together. Somehow, whenever they were together it was as if the world conspired to make it easy.

They had both slept little and once the train started moving, they leaned into each other and fell asleep. Again, they were both aware of the familiarity of their bodies, like old friends. They woke as the train drew into Figueras. They disembarked and followed the signs to the bus station. They had two hours to wait. They bought tickets and crammed their bags into a left luggage locker before setting off through the town to the Dali museum.

Figueras was parched and empty. There were signs of a festival, canopies of paper bunting over the streets and squares. The Dali museum was seething with tourists and vendors of Dali tat. It wasn't where they wanted to be. They walked back to the main square, found a café with seats on the pavement where they could eat an early lunch before taking the bus to Cadaqués.

The bus took them through some grim new towns before snaking up into the hills that shrouded the coast from their view. They were treated to momentary glimpses of an enticingly blue Mediterranean Sea before it disappeared behind hills covered with dried up olive trees and cactuses that thrust huge phallic flowers to the sky. They passed the highest point of their journey and the bus wound down a series of tight hairpins into Cadaqués. It was late afternoon when they arrived and they set off immediately in search of a room, so they could leave their things and take to the sea. It didn't take long for them to realise that every hotel was full. It was the beginning of a long weekend and the town was full of tourists and weekenders from the city cruising along the winding road that marked the junction of town and sea. Their search was thorough and, within an hour, they knew every hotel, bar and restaurant in Cadaqués.

They also knew it was pointless to go on, but they'd found the bar they wanted to return to that night, the restaurant with the finest view of the sea and their favourite hotel where they made a reservation for the next available room. It was easy to accept their first night together on the beach; their meeting was fated and fate had given them a night under the stars. They took what they needed for the night, stowed the rest in a loft above the bar and ordered two mojitos, blended by a cantinero from Milan, from three different rums, brown sugar, lime and fresh mint. As the sun set over the sea, they took their drinks down to the water's edge and drank one toast to the angel, one to each other and one to their first day together.

IV   Venice VCE

Serendipity brought them from Spain, along the French Riviera and across Italy to Venice. Wherever they went they were welcomed. There was a magic in their being together, people were drawn to it, wanted to bathe in it, wanted to contribute to it. Their journey was free and spontaneous. They visited beautiful beaches, ancient towns, an artist colony, built into the remains of a medieval village, shattered by an earthquake a hundred years before.

Their last night was spent in Venice and they celebrated and mourned over a picnic in their decadent hotel room. In the space contained by its peeling walls, the blossoming of their love left an indelible impression on the atmosphere, an atmosphere which, unbeknown to them, would seduce lovers from around the world for years to come. They drank local wine and ate sweet roasted peppers and anchovies preserved in oil. They fed each other olives and slices of tomato and figs and other ripe fruits gathered from the early morning market. They remembered their imminent parting and their hot tears washed the juices from the feast and from their bodies into the bed. They promised themselves to each other. They promised to wait. They promised to take this gift and make it grow. The made love and slept. They woke up and packed their bags.

They slept again, lightly, aware of the contact of their bodies, aware of the morning light outside their room, aware of the joy and the pain, the finding and the losing.

Too soon it was time to leave. They took their bags and left the hotel for the empty streets. They found an open café, and drank caffè corretto at the bar with the few others who shared the street at this hour. They took the bus out of town, over the bridge that separated the magic of Venice from the ordinary world. They entered the small airport. She checked in. They both hoped that something would be wrong with her ticket, that she would have to stay, that fate would not separate them now. They didn't mention it to each other. Then they waited, that awful waiting that airports create, in lounges, in halls, in queues, in aircraft, life on hold, waiting to say goodbye, when there are so many other things to say that cannot be said because of that pending goodbye.

It was time for her to go. It was almost a relief and yet, it was the last thing either of them wanted. Then she was gone and still there was more waiting to do. Now they couldn't see each other or touch each other but they were both still here, close but invisible to each other. He stepped outside into the heat and the sunshine; the airport was already too busy. He clung to the fence, watching the runway, waiting for her plane to pass by, now longing for it to leave so he would know that she was really gone and not just invisible. At last her plane taxied by.

He wanted to see her face but he couldn't see anything at the windows, couldn't see if she was watching him, couldn't see if she was waving, couldn't see if, like him, she was crying.

As her plane took off his silent tears drenched his face. He found a bench beside the canal and lay down, waiting for the time when his plane would take him away from this place which he hated now. He drifted between awake and dream. In every dream she was there, just as usual, without symbol, without significance, just simply there, with him, as he knew she should be.

V   London LGW

It was a month since their separation. They'd talked every day on the phone. She was coming to London, her first trip to his city. They had only three days. As he waited at the airport he was scared. He was scared that he'd made it all up. Perhaps it was just a holiday romance after all. Perhaps he wouldn't remember her or she him or they would look at each other and know it should have ended in Venice.

He'd booked a room in a hotel near where he lived. He wasn't ready for her to see his apartment. He wanted her to see only the person she met in Barcelona, naked, undefined by his home, by his possessions, his books and his ways of being at home. He felt that she'd seen the truest version of himself and he wanted to know that he could still hold on to that in his own city. His apartment carried a record of the years, of other loves and disappointments, of celebrations and depressions, of life changes and stagnations. He felt like she'd seen the flower and he didn't yet want her to see the dirt. He checked the display. Her plane was on time and he headed for the arrivals lounge.

She gazed down from her window at the new landscape below, this little land she'd never seen before and yet imagined living in. Now she felt excited. When she left, she was full of uncertainty.

Her memories had been tainted by the advice of her friends. They'd all told her to forget him, that it was just a holiday romance, that they were always doomed to fail. She began to believe them, convinced herself that she'd come just to prove them right, just to clear the fantasy from her mind. Now she was so close, she knew they were wrong. She knew that her friends could never understand the love she'd found.

She remembered her arrival in Rome. How could she ever have guessed what was in store for her. She remembered the dancer and her words: "Regret nothing, lest it be for the best." She remembered the flight out of Venice airport, watching her lover in his white linen shirt, standing behind the fence, unable to see her waving, blowing kisses, crying.

At last the plane touched down. That awful month of waiting was over. She drifted through the endless corridors that led her through immigration, baggage claim and customs, and stepped out into the hordes of expectant faces squeezed behind the barricades. She saw only one face, the face of her lover, waiting, beautiful as ever. She wanted to abandon her trolley and run. She was constrained by convention until she reached him. She leapt into his arms, buried herself into the feel of his body, his smell, his breath, covered his face with kisses and tears, gave her body, took his body, felt herself hot with desire, wanting to take him now, to undress him now, to feel her nakedness against his nakedness.

She was oblivious to the rest of the world, to the people jostling to pass them. She was back with her lover.

VI   New York JFK

She had an hour to wait for her plane. It was now six months since they'd met. Her life had changed completely. She'd changed completely. She thought of her lover, of the times they had spent together in his city, in her city. She thought of the long weekend she'd spent with him in a hotel in London, when she'd first seen him in his own environment, met his friends, visited his favourite bars and restaurants and parks, when she realised how deeply she loved him, when she realised how much she wanted to leave New York. She remembered the times he'd come to stay with her in New York. She thought of the days she passed, sitting in her office, waiting to leave, waiting to spend the night with him, of the days he spent waiting for her to leave, sitting in her apartment, writing, walking the streets, telling her stories of his days.

She bought a coffee and went outside, to the corner by the wall, where they sat and smoked together while they waited for his flight. He said he would build a little garden here, with plants and flowers and chairs, just for lovers, waiting to say good-bye. She remembered so many partings and so many meetings, so many trips to airports, so many moments of pure joy as he finally arrived, so many awful waits when he was due to leave. She remembered the weeks of longing after they'd separated once again, the difficulty of sleeping alone again, the difficulty of finding a life alone again. She remembered the weeks of anticipation when he'd booked a flight, of counting the days, of wishing the days away. She checked the time. It was time to leave. She went back into the terminal and walked towards the gate. Now there would be no more waiting, no more meetings and partings, no more longings and anticipations.

VII   London LHR

He was restless the entire night, excited and also, if he dared to admit it, fearful. He couldn't say what made him scared. It was just a feeling, a cloying feeling that emerged from somewhere deep inside his flesh. He pushed it away with his imaginings of the days that lay ahead. He'd been preparing for weeks for her to finally see his home. He'd bought new bed sheets and pillows. He'd cleaned every corner of his home, discarding untidy piles of paper that normally filled his life. He'd bought sweet smelling flowers and incense and Champagne. He'd found fresh blackberries imported from some poor country in South America. He'd chased the heavy smell of tobacco smoke from his rooms and now, at last, in the dark of this early morning he could give full vent to his longing. He'd rationed the moments of his wanting for a whole month, knowing that given into, it would overwhelm him. Now he had time to be overwhelmed, just a little time, before he set off to the airport.

He was aware of being awake at four and then being shocked out of his dream at six, when the telephone rang with the matronly voice of his reminder call. He'd been dreaming. It was hard to leave it behind. He was on a large boat, a pleasure boat, sometimes like one of those that imprisoned party goers in its oppressive metal discotheque as it voyaged aimlessly up the Thames, sometimes grander and more elegant, reminiscent of one from a scene in an old movie set in Louisiana. The boat was full of friends and many other people besides, strange people, some in drag or in fancy dress, circus performers aiming to shock with grotesque tricks. He was searching for someone, but he didn't know who.

He passed through many rooms, some simply bare metal boxes, others gorgeously decorated with fine fabrics and gilded furniture. He found a pool, an enormous swimming pool. He wondered how they could fit such a large pool inside the boat. He was pulled into the pool, pulled under the water by a woman dressed as a clown. He had no fear, no need to breathe. He went deeper and deeper, willingly, still searching. He emerged from the surface of the water which was now a little pool on the deck of the boat. He saw that the boat had entered a narrow canal which stretched steeply down into the ocean. They gathered speed. There was an excitement aboard. He knew that when they reached the ocean, the boat would continue down beneath the water. Now he was scared.

He stepped out of his bed and the memory of the dream clung to him. He made a coffee and ran the bath, sank into the heat of the water, prepared his body for his lover. He washed away the dream and washed away the pain of waiting for his lover to arrive. He used sandalwood soap to purify his aura and a new razor to shave his face.

He used conditioner on his hair and moisturiser on his skin and rubbed her favourite perfume deep into his neck and chest. He put on a fresh white linen shirt, dark trousers and shoes and the soft grey cashmere jacket that she said she loved. The phone rang. His taxi was waiting and he hurried down the stairs to start his journey. The sun had just risen and traffic was light. The journey out to Heathrow was fast and magical. The morning light glowed on the mist that haunted the ground beside the road. The driver talked. He told of his life travelling as a courier, of the weeks waiting in expensive hotels in so many cities, waiting to carry a package, perhaps a diamond or a document, to another city, another hotel, another wait. He talked of driving a truck across America before he met his wife. He talked of life in New York with his wife and how he drove a yellow cab and made three hundred dollars a night. He talked of how they moved back to London, of how they both worked nights so that they could spend the days together.

At Heathrow he paid his driver and added some more for his stories. He checked the arrival time and went to the restaurant for breakfast. Now he could enjoy the wait, enjoy playing with his longing, knowing that soon it would be rewarded. Her flight landed on time and he waited. The baggage in hall indicator appeared and he slowly strolled down to the arrival lounge and found himself a place behind the rail. He waited. He watched as clutches of people emerged from the customs hall. He watched the meetings and greetings, the passionate embraces and clumsy kisses, the moments of excitement and moments of embarrassment, the tears and laughter. His excitement increased, waiting to see his lover's face, waiting to gather her in his arms, waiting to release the containment of his desire, waiting to smell her, to taste her, to feel her. He waited an hour. He gave it ten minutes more, then another ten, then ten more. He went to the airline desk. They couldn't tell him where she was. He found a phone from where he could watch. He called her number. He got an answer machine. It wasn't her voice; it was a man's voice. He called her work number. There was no answer, no familiar voicemail, just ringing. He called his own number, entered the code for the message machine. There were no messages. He tried all of the numbers again. It was the same. He went back to the barrier and waited some more. He went to the information desk. No, she was not held by immigration. No, she was not held by customs. No, they couldn't give details of who was on the flight.

VIII   Rome FCO

The plane plunged through the bright early morning light and juddered to a halt on the rough tarmac of Fiumicino airport. She stepped out into the sunshine and down the stairs. She took deep breaths of Italian air. She was filled with a sense of freedom after the long cramped flight from New York. Her body trembled slightly with an anticipation of something unknown.

She waited calmly by the wing of the aircraft before stepping onto the bus just as the doors closed, assuring herself of an unimpeded view of the short trip to the airport buildings. Once inside, she waited at the carousel, oblivious to the hordes of tired travellers jostling for position. A space cleared around her, a quiet space that nobody wanted to invade. She collected her bag and passed easily through immigration, receiving nothing more than an approving glance from the official. Customs waved her past and she stepped through the doors into the arrival lounge. Her friend was waiting for her, an elegant woman with a long straight dancer's neck. They embraced and stepped out into the sunlight to the car that was waiting to take them away. At last she felt she was where she belonged.

IX   London LHR

He went back to the phone and tried all the numbers again. When he got through to his answer machine there was a message from his lover.

"My love, I'm sorry, I'm in Rome, I'm not coming to London, I can't really explain, we'll talk some time, I love you, thanks for everything you gave me."

He wanted to die. He bought some cigarettes. He knew it was slow, but perhaps he liked to wait after all. He stepped out of the airport and sat on the concrete by the luggage trolleys. He lit a cigarette. Now he knew, finally knew, there was no God, no fate, no order. Now he knew there was only chance, that the universe was so complex that sometimes, it was bound to look like there was order. Now he finally knew that all his stories were just a way to keep insecurity at bay, just a way to make him feel that he had some power, some influence, some value. Now he knew that nothing really mattered. He felt free.

A woman appeared, standing, looking down at him. She wanted to join him; she didn't know why. She wanted a cigarette. She didn't smoke but today she wanted to smoke. She had just arrived from Rome. This was her first time in London. She had gone to Rome to meet her lover. He wasn't there to meet her. She waited.

While she waited, she met a woman, a beautiful woman who looked like a dancer but said she was an actress. She was drawn to the woman, felt safe beside her, trusted her in a world she could no longer trust. The woman said she should be in London; that was where she belonged. She believed her. There was nothing else to believe. She took the next flight to London. Could they share a taxi?

The Habit

In memory of Stanley Keleman

Although the nuns had long since departed, the current owners maintained the connection with the divine. They were a rather dull and desiccated little group that welcomed him at the garden gate. They insisted on showing him their meditation room before he could see his bedroom. It was a large and musty space with a floor of polished old wood edged with piles of well-used cushions in various faded pastel colours. At one end was a shrine with a photograph of an old man who evoked no association, and a couple of brass bowls filled with rice and water and burned out incense.

They had made it clear in the brochure that, although the meditation was not compulsory, they did encourage their visitors to take advantage of the morning sittings. Nothing about them nor the room encouraged him, but he nodded in feigned appreciation as they renewed their offer.

After a brief tour of the rest of the house, he was finally shown to his room in a converted stable block, hidden from the main house by a tangle of hedge. His guide on this part of the tour told him how the nuns had converted the block long ago and it still retained "the special atmosphere of their devotion".

At last, he was left alone. As his host's footsteps receded down the stairs, he unpacked his bag. He was one of the first to arrive for the workshop and, as yet, the stable block was empty but for him. By the time he had hung his clothes in the wardrobe and arranged his books on the desk, he was overcome by the effects of a too early start, and the long journey from Amsterdam.

He lay down on the narrow bed and gave himself to sleep. As his body settled and relaxed, the images held in the tension of its tissue released and raced across his mind in clouds, unconnected clouds without obvious meaning, clouds of memory stored within a system unknown to his waking mind.

The clouds cleared and the image of his room appeared from behind the veil, not the image that he closed his eyes to but another, from another time. Where once was the wardrobe, that now contained his clothes, was a small desk, rough and poorly finished. On the desk stood a single candle stick and a book bound in black leather. The thin light from the candle was all that lit the room. The window from which he had gazed onto the vegetable garden had not yet been constructed.

A movement drew his attention to the corner of the room where he had arranged his books and papers on the desk. A figure stepped forward from the dusk - the figure of a nun, cloaked from the crown of her head to the ground in loose black fabric.

She drew back the cover from her face and showed her pale beauty, a beauty barely touched by the sun, her features marked only by the divine, radiant and impassioned.

She released the clasp at her throat and the fabric slipped away, leaving her standing naked in the pool of her dark cover. By the candlelight, her white skin glowed, outwitting the brightness of the flame. By now he was sitting on the bed, transfixed by the woman who stood before him, his eyes seduced by the untainted perfection of her form. He reached out, but withdrew, discouraged by the gentle shake of her head which caused her dark hair to unfurl from the loose twist at the back of her neck. The soft smile of her eyes and lips reassured him and he sat back, content to receive, accepting not to take.

He watched as her hands ran through her hair and unwound long curls, which dropped across her shoulders and breasts. He watched as her tender hands explored and caressed the shape and form of her own body. Small shivers and tremors of excitement raced across her muscles. He watched as she touched places as if they had never been touched before. He watched as her hands formed a pair that glided down over her breasts and belly to the darkness of her pubic hair.

Small shivers and tremors of excitement raced across his muscles. Heat and the weightlessness of anticipation fevered his belly.

He saw the flash of a golden wedding ring as her hands plunged deep between her legs, and the room filled with the odour of her passion, like wood smoke and musk. The smell dilated his nostrils and inflated his lungs and his arms stretched forward to meet hands that glistened with her own juices. Before they touched, her image washed away in the sunlight burning through the window that had reopened behind him.

Voices in the corridor challenged his understanding of what was real. The wardrobe was there, as was the desk with his books and papers. The smell too was still there, as real as the passion in his belly.

His host led two women past the open door. The second woman's glance extended beyond a moment and he blushed, certain he saw her sniff the air, certain of her faint and familiar smile. He didn't see her again until the introductory session late in the afternoon. He arrived late, his sense of time lost in reverie as he showered and dressed, his interest in the workshop lost to the wish to see his visitor again.

He was the last to enter the room and found his place on a cushion in the middle of the group. He could more easily have taken a chair, but he felt as if the eyes of the older man who led the group could see right through him, and he preferred to hide behind a row of heads.

The subject was 'intimacy', but he heard little, distracted as he was by a furtive search for the face he had seen through the door. He hadn't found her before the first exercise was proposed. He followed the old man's softly spoken instructions and held his face in his hands.

"Let your hands feel your face... Make your hands soft and receptive... Receive your face into your open hands... Let your face soften... Give your face to your hands..."

Tears welled in his eyes and soaked his fingers. The scent of wood smoke and musk seemed to emerge from the wetness. His chest tightened to hold in the gasp and sob that struggled to erupt from his body. He lost the struggle when he heard a gasp and sob from somewhere close and his lungs emptied out their grief into his hands.

The inhalation that followed was filled with the same familiar scent, now no longer from the wetness of his fingers, but from the air beyond. The exercise was brought to its conclusion and he opened his eyes. She unfurled her dark hair from its loose twist at the back of her neck and sent another wave of wood smoke and musk his way.

The session finished and she turned towards him, her face still wet with tears. She followed him to his room. As she undressed, her gold wedding ring flashed in the evening light from the window.

We were three again

From STILL, published 2019

When Judith and I entered the inner quadrangle of the monastery we found the space empty but for one young monk, motionless, suspended in the act of lighting the butter lamps. Hawa, Rafiq and Mariam had done their work with their usual elegance, waiting for the boy to light the final lamp and extinguish the taper before they unfolded stillness across the courtyard.

The soft light of the butter lamps flickered in the boy's green eyes as they gazed into another place. The only other movement was from a cat, a white and marmalade cat, wearing a necklace of roughly polished turquoise. For a moment a wave of anxiety flowed through me. The cat was untouched by the stillness. This cat belonged to no man. If she belonged her consciousness would be tied to her owner. But the cat was not owned. The cat was a free spirit and presented a threat to our plan. It is easy to kill a cat but, thankfully, I afforded her a moment's grace and discovered she was with us, a spy who had retained this furry form just for this moment. That is, of course, the beauty of the cat, their ability to gaze between worlds and times and wait for the perfect moment. Cat came to me, twirled her long tail around my ankle and led me to one of the buildings. She whispered to me. "All the others are in here, there is a puja. A wealthy man has died and the family can afford to pay them all to chant, to help his soul become free."

Inside, the entire community sat frozen, suspended in time. Although the rice grains had fallen to the floor, many young hands remained in the air, still in the act of throwing rice. Others held sticks, poised to strike their bells and chimes, and others held their lips to silent trumpets and horns.

All, just like the butter lamp boy, gazed into another place. All, that is, except for the abbot. His eyes followed us, even if his body remained held in stillness. I could feel the intention in his gaze. It was ugly, dark and mean, no longer hidden from the world by the veil of well-rehearsed kindness he had learned to portray with his body and smile. His darkness was held in check by his incapacity to reach into his robes and wrap his fingers around the bronze double dorje that had passed through the hands of a long line of abbots practised in the art of darkness and deception.

I took it for myself and I plucked a few gems from within the subtle threads of his energy body. I could feel a little of his darkness touch me and I felt a cruel joy as I looked into his eyes and saw evil with no power. I resisted the temptation to gloat, once I saw that he had nothing more to tell me. I turned away, back to Judith and the cat.

"He cannot help us. He has spent his entire life here, and played the role of the abbot for years, but he is still nothing more than the discipline master. The only tools he ever used were the smile and the whip. The double dorje was wasted on a man with no protection against stillness. There is another. Somewhere here there is another but I cannot feel his breath."

Hawa, Rafiq and Mariam had joined us. Mariam told us that the rest of our family was already searching the monastery. She warned us that time was not on our side. "Winged messengers have already flown from the roofs. Herve plucked many of them from the sky but some escaped - an eagle's claws are no match for dragonflies and bees and he needed to concentrate on more important things. He said to tell you Kali is well. She knows you're here."

Tears welled in my eyes and I started to reach out to her. "Not yet," Mariam said as she seized my wrist and hauled my attention back to the moment.

"We need you here. There is still too much unknown and Juan, Mireille and Alice are already preparing her."

"I need a second or two," I said and sank cross-legged to the stone floor. I passed the double dorje to Judith.

"Hold this, you might need it."

Cat sat beside me and tuned her purr to my breath.

With Judith and the stillness workers watching over us, I closed my eyes and turned my attention to my fingertips. They touched the floor and felt the familiarity of the stone. I looked back to when Christopher and I sat side by side in this room, both young monks with little to do but repeat the prayers and wait for the moment to throw some rice. Then, as now, it was the discipline master who dressed like the abbot and led the prayers. Now, as then, the true abbot lived as the slenderest thread of life, within a body slowly killed and preserved through a daily draught of tree lacquer. I stood and faced the discipline master and felt a wave of appreciation for the role he played - the most difficult role in this monastery, balancing pure love with an equally pure evil, outwardly wearing the role of the abbot but inwardly obliged to subsume all goodness, all aspiration and all hope. Even as he sat, held in stillness, I caught the faintest flicker of a smile in his eyes and I felt his love.

I turned around towards the altar and passed through the curtain into a long corridor, with its row of teak caskets lining one wall. We opened each to reveal a lineage of lignified abbots. Once the last thread of life had departed their bodies, they were undressed, painted and polished, so that each had the same sheen as the wooden box in which he had sat for the last seven years of his life. Each body was then dressed in the rainbow colours that celebrated their achievement.

When we reached the end of the line, we found the last box open and the current abbot sitting there. Just the faintest flicker in the air betrayed the fact that he had not yet departed and I quickly clasped my hand over his fontanelle to prevent him from doing so. I could feel the gap where his practice had opened the bones and the membrane trembling from just the slightest murmur of life within.

Through the careful consumption of tree lacquer, and the practice of esoteric techniques revealed to very few, he had gradually withdrawn his life from his body, layer by layer replacing his own fluids with the lacquer, effectively mummifying himself from the outside in. All that remained of the abbot was concentrated in the thread of fluid that reached from his heart to the centre of his brain and was already pushing against the membranes - the last barrier to his total freedom.

Although my light contact was enough to hold him in place, the fury contained was immense, the fury of many lifetimes of dedication that had brought him to this place, to the edge of freedom from birth, to a return to the source.

That fury began to scramble my thoughts, brought panic to my breathing and sweat to my skin. I replaced my hand with an old bronze ceremonial bowl that Judith brought from the altar, and breathed a sigh of relief, as I was able to put a little more space between the abbot and me.

This was the great irony of the practice, that such a strong will could still be contained by such a small resistance. It was why the monastery was hidden from the world and protected against disturbance. We were lucky to arrive in time, the abbot was close to completion, and the force of his leaving would have sent a huge wave of energy through this, his last refuge. At such moments, there were earthquakes and rock falls and the monks lived with this risk, knowing that if they survived, their own status would be raised enormously as they bathed in the pure rainbow light of the passing abbot.

Cat touched me again with her tail, and her whisper reminded me of the tunnel that lay beneath the abbot. Carefully, we slid his casket to one side and opened an entrance into the stony darkness. Cat led the way down a spiral stairway, cut through solid rock, until we emerged onto a familiar terrace. Above us loomed the outer wall of the monastery and below us, a sheer cliff that seemed to plunge forever. Suspended on that cliff was Kali, sitting in her cell. I knew this terrace from a dream. I knew this terrace as the place I stood arguing with Christopher. And yet still, I could not understand. The rest of our family joined us on the terrace. Cat told me of the Vril tunnels, deep in the rock below us, inaccessible from the monastery, and too small for any but the Vril. She had never seen them herself, but knew of them from other creatures that lived in the monastery. The tunnels were used for the construction of the cell in which Kali now sat.

Cat knew of one other tunnel and showed me the place where it opened onto the terrace.

"They use it to blow smoke into the beehive, to sedate the bees in times of transition. The herbs they use are on a shelf in the main kitchen."

She knew no more. A cat needed so much brain for action, it didn't have much to spare for memory or mind. It was time for the dreaming bone. I took it from my pocket and my family gathered around me, in part to hold me as I dreamed, in part to share that dream. I slipped the bone onto my finger and let my body soften into the warm embrace of the body of my family. The dream came quickly, vividly, so much confusion cleared simply by being back in this place.

I saw again the scene with Christopher on the terrace and heard the argument clearly. We were brothers, one of us tasked to die and one of us tasked to kill. He was to die. I was to kill.

For our entire lives in this monastery we had prepared for this moment and now I refused. Above us, the fifth abbot was about to die. I could hear the puja building to that zenith. What would complete the process was our action. Our abbot was ready to leave forever. The energy accumulated by his sacrifice would bless the entire sangha. All that was needed was for Christopher and me to fulfil our roles. I was to kill and he was to die. He was to die willingly and I was to kill freely.

Our entire lives we had prepared, and I failed. He was to stand on the edge of the terrace and I was to push. And I refused. His action was needed to complete the action of the abbot. His action would liberate the abbot forever and raise the status of the entire sangha. His action would guarantee his own rebirth as the seventh abbot of this monastery. My action would lead me to the role of the discipline master - outwardly playing the role of the abbot, inwardly embodying the forces of evil and love, wielding the smile and the whip. And I failed. I hadn't yet learned how to kill.

And now I saw that cat was wrong, a wealthy man had not died. A poor man with nothing, not even a body, was about to die. The puja suspended in time above us was for the abbot. Now he sat with a singing bowl trapping his soul in his body as I dreamed.

And I saw how I failed. And I saw how I fled. And I saw how the fifth abbot had been left incomplete. And now I knew where to find the old lama, trapped once again in his lignified body. And I saw how I ran. And I saw the lifetimes I was obliged to return over and over to learn how to kill. And I saw how finally, in this life, I had learned how to kill.

And I saw how the system was changed, how my failure then had led to what was unfolding now, how the price I had to pay was the life of Kali, the woman who sat poised between life and death in the cell suspended on the cliff wall far below. And I saw that what saved me from Christopher's death blow was not luck nor intuition, but the sound of a small gold coin thrown from the parapet above by Kali, the secret consort to the abbot.

And now I knew how she had loved me then, and nurtured me through many lives since then, and found me once again in this life, and loved me and taught me how to kill, knowing it was her I would finally have to kill. And now I turned to the details, and I saw the Vril within their tunnels, fires ready to burn the slender poles on which balanced Kali's cell. And I understood what I saw when Herve first took me to look at the cell, that crafty construction that ensured that the structure would fail, and the walls would fall away, moments before Kali's seat itself would topple.

And I saw how she sat and prepared for that moment, when she would fall head-first through space, gazing out across the mountains, willingly giving up her soul as the abbot gave up his. And I saw that she had to do it - it was the price she would pay for her love of me. And I knew that it had to happen.

When I opened my eyes, we all knew the role we had to play. The light workers remained on the terrace while the rest of us returned to the abbots' corridor. I stopped at the last and put my hand to his heart and assured him that all would be well. Hawa remained with him ready to remove the bowl from his head. Rafiq and Mariam followed cat to the kitchen to fetch the herbs.

I stopped at the fifth abbot and brought my brow to his brow. I felt the faintest stirrings of the old lama within. I removed the gold coin that covered his fontanelle and put it in my pocket. When I stepped back from behind the altar, Juan, Mireille and Alice had already found places amongst the monks. They were ready to lean on the sound to help make up for lost time. I found myself face to face with the discipline master, and bowed to him in honour of the difficulty of his role. Although he hadn't yet had to kill to take this place, he was ready for the task. It was he who would tell the Vril to light the fires that would send Kali to her death - a hands-off killing, much easier than in my day. I returned the double dorje to its place in his robes. He would need it to send the signal to the Vril. I didn't return the jewels I stole from him. It didn't work that way.

Rafiq and Mariam returned with the herbs, a tightly packed bundle held together with a red silk thread. They had already set it smouldering on the fire in the kitchen and, for a moment, I let its smoke carry my prayers to the altar before I returned to the terrace. The stillness workers would remain with the sangha. They had a difficult task - to remove stillness without accident and control each individual's flow of time until we reached unison.

On the terrace I dropped the bundle of smouldering herbs down the hole and could feel the slight breeze that would draw its smoke to the bees and sedate them before the stillness was removed.

I joined Judith on the ledge and gazed down at the roof of Kali's cell, directly below us. I could see Herve soaring below. Robert and Remi were gazing into the light. We could not afford to lose track of each other.

"Ready?"

I turned to Judith in an embrace. I could feel the stillness receding. The music resumed, momentarily chaotic, but soon called into order by the sound workers' voices that were so pure, so beautiful, so in harmony, that it felt as if they could bring order into everything. Now I held Judith's hand and we waited. The stillness was gone but another stillness took its place - a rightful stillness, poised, anticipating. The music worked its inevitable way to its zenith - order and time restored by the sound workers. The abbot pressed more forcefully against the last soft spot in his fontanelle, now freed from the pressure of the singing bowl.

I took from my pocket one of the jewels I had taken from the discipline master and integrated its knowledge into my web. I felt his hand rise and strike the stone with the double dorje. I felt the fine resonance that touched the Vril and told them it was time to light the fires.

I saw the jets of white smoke either side of Kali's cell, as The Winds from the North poured through the Vril tunnels, driving furnaces that consumed the poles. The music stopped.

All that remained was the unified 'om' of the stillness workers - now no longer with the monks, but here beside us on the ledge. The smoke turned to black and the walls fell away from Kali's cell. Herve swooped towards her. The abbot's soul broke through the final membrane. The stones of the monastery began to shake with the force. Judith and I dropped headfirst from the ledge, releasing our hands just as Kali dropped sideways from her seat, hands outstretched to meet our hands. We were three again, our vision as clear as diamond. The stillness workers slowed us for the moments I needed to heal her heart, and then we were one.

We followed Herve's direction and saw where he was leading us - first just a softening in the light, then a pattern in the air that didn't belong, then a Vril-hole that opened out beneath us. We glided our way in, followed by the others, all now hand in hand in their threes.

The cold rushing air of the high Himalayas become soft and warm and viscid. Gravity exerted no force in the Vril-hole and our fall slowed to a soft and gentle caress. Hands reached out and three became twelve - a circle suspended in space and time. Warm air between our toes gave way to soft grass and earth, and twelve became thirteen as we stood in a circle around the old lama, in the High Atlas mountain retreat that Hawa, Rafiq and Mariam had prepared for us so long before.

Love

Inspired by Truth

It was nine years since she saw that little wooden box. Nine years during which she buried her love beneath the heaviness of an overwhelming marriage, as she had buried that box deep beneath other boxes, unopened boxes that contained the colourful fabrics and cushions, pictures and souvenirs of her former life.

Now she lived a colourless life, imprisoned by walls painted in expensive earth colours. The same colours as her neighbours' walls, bought from the same shop as her neighbours' paint by the same interior designer.

Nine years she lived this caricature of a life, hoping to forget, hoping to forget that former life, to forget that former love, to forget the box buried beneath boxes in the attic, high up in this prison of a house, in an attic above rooms she never cared to visit since she first moved in.

Nine years she lived with a man she had grown to loathe. Nine years she pretended to enjoy his company, pretended to be impressed by his achievements, learned to smile a false smile that fitted so well in the world of false smiles to which he belonged.

Nine years she stood by his side, dressed the way he liked, smelled the way he liked, cooked the way he liked and kept their home the way the interior designer intended.

Nine years she slept beside him, although as far apart as the bed would permit. Nine years she closed and vacated her body, so he could fuck her when he wanted. Nine years she pretended she wanted his child but killed her eggs with her thoughts, disgusted by the idea of bringing another of her husband's achievements into the world.

Nine years had passed and nothing he said, nothing he bought, nowhere he took her, nobody she ever met, could clear her heart of the man she loved, the man who died in her arms, the man who left his broken body in her bed as his beautiful and pure soul caressed and kissed her as he left.

And now she stood in the kitchen, cursing the latest egg embedded into her womb. A perfect embryo, carefully selected by experts who harvested her ovaries as if she were a cow, who guaranteed to take the best of her and the best of him, and make the perfect son for a man who believed he had the right to buy everything. And she let her darkness and loathing saturate her womb and drive out any hope of nourishment or love until, as she leaned against the granite worktop, she felt the first contraction and the heat of blood running down her legs.

And through the pain and the relief and the satisfaction of seeing blood on the wood of the kitchen floor she knew she could not do this again. She knew she could no longer live this lie.

And she let the blood flow free and mark her journey drop by drop through the floors of this home she so hated, past the bedroom that would never see her raped again, past the nursery that would never be a prison to her child, past the guest rooms into which she never could bear to invite a guest, past the staff bedrooms, deserted by servants who stole her last pleasures, shopping for fruit in the market or tending the garden.

And each floor she passed carried the stain of her blood. And each floor she passed felt like a journey back to herself, through doors she thought she had closed forever, into layers of memories she thought she would never see again.

And finally, she reached the door to the attic and her hesitation was marked by one last thick clot. She had never been through this door. As she opened it, she felt light pour into a room long shuttered within her mind.

And when she climbed the steep stairs, she could see that the movers had done exactly as she asked, consigning her entire past to this hidden floor. On the far wall, away from the pool of light that shone through the sky light, stood a stack of boxes, each labelled by her with a different colour, each containing precious things from a different room: from the sitting room where she sat with him when he first came back to her, from the kitchen where she prepared his coffee with beans bought for him from the Algerian coffee shop, from the bathroom where she washed him and inspected him and cleaned his wounds each time he came back to her, from the bedroom where she watched over him and protected him from his memories and fears, and where he died in her arms. And where, as he died, he taught her how to love.

Without interest, she took down the wall of boxes one by one, until she found his box. It was the only one unmarked, at the bottom of the wall, stuffed with cushions to protect another box, never opened since the day the police brought it to her.

"His possessions", they said. Possessions she never thought to look for after he died and his body was taken away from her. The documents were found in his jacket and the key led to a safe deposit box which they had emptied of its contents.

"There was nothing suspicious", they said, "nothing to be pursued. No indication of a next of kin." Which left her as the person to whom to bring his things. She didn't want to open the box, had no wish to know more about him now that he was gone, only wanted to hold him tightly, forever, wrapped in the muscle of her heart, that still skipped a beat each time she thought of him.

She packed the box, along with all her possessions, the week he died. She put everything into storage, and stayed with her sister until her flat was sold. She pretended to be courted by her sister's boss, a man whose wealth could swallow her up and whose vanity would never permit him to see beyond the facade she presented. He was convinced he had finally won her, as he did with everything he wanted. She wanted to be possessed. She wanted to be dominated. She wanted to be consumed. Better that than to be flayed alive by grief.

In her bedroom she packed the box in a small suitcase with some clothes, some cash, some toiletries. She took nothing else, not her jewels nor photos, none of it felt like it belonged to her. The cash was no problem, she'd earned that anyway.

She closed the front door one last time, leaving her keys inside. She cut roses and took a taxi to leave them on his grave. "I'm ready", she said, "to find out who you are".

She checked into a suite at her husband's club and asked to be left alone. It was the kind of club that would keep her secret from her husband, as much as it would hide his secrets from her.

Coincidence put her in the same room where he arrogantly had his way with her and she returned his greed with a performance she never knew she could muster.

She summoned a lover and was happy to know her skill in that domain had not diminished over the years. He was available for her just as he had always been. She never asked, but she always knew when he had left another lover in her favour. He arrived on time, freshly washed and shaved, bearing gifts of wine and fruit as usual. A decade had not cost him his looks. If anything, he looked better for the smattering of grey hairs at his temples and the softening of the skin around his neck and chin. He asked nothing of her, nothing about the last nine years, and nothing about tomorrow.

He did not disappoint. He called her back into her body with his touch - softened her, moistened her, opened her, entered her, responded to her call to enter deeper. And he held her like this, free from demands, free from expectations until, at last, she let go of the knots she had tied in her womb to keep her husband away from all that was most precious. And they lay like this until the tears streamed freely from her eyes and it was time to ask him to go.

When she woke late in the morning, she asked the concierge to book her a flight to New York and a suite in her husband's preferred hotel.

She knew she would no longer be travelling in secret. But she also knew her husband would not force her to return. He was predictable and would wait in the expectation of her coming back, before cutting her off from everything he thought mattered in life. How could a man like him know how little all that meant to her!

In her hotel room, with its views over Central Park, she carefully, slowly, ritually, laid out the contents of his box on the bed. In the centre was the card he gave her, with the contact number of the photographer's wife. In the first circle around the card she arranged nine rolls of unprocessed film. In the next circle, she laid two passports side by side, his watch, a small leather bag which contained a palmful of gold dirhams, a Byzantine cross made of pewter, softened by the touch of many hands, prayer beads, a simple bronze key.

The passports revealed two different lands, two different birthdays, two different family names. The first name, the one that mattered most because it was all she ever knew him by, was the same on both.

She called the photographer's wife and explained herself. It didn't take long; she had been expecting her call for years. She walked through the park to the Upper West Side building the photographer's wife had described.

The doorman called ahead to announce her arrival and directed her across the courtyard, past the fountain, to the far corner where she found the lift.

When the lift stopped, she could see a woman waiting on the other side of the latticed gate. She expected to exchange places as the gate opened but the woman gathered her into an embrace.

"Oh, it is you!" She said. "I so hoped it would be, and I was afraid this moment might never come. Please come in but prepare yourself for a surprise."

The photographer's wife opened the door to the apartment and bade her enter first. She followed her in, waiting close behind, perhaps afraid she might faint and be in need of catching.

She faced herself across the hall, twelve years younger, stepping ashore from an old Greek ferry. It was an amazing photograph, taken from a distance, capturing a moment of extraordinary aliveness in the life of a young women. She was walking down the ramp alone, but all eyes were on her: the boat crew, the stevedores, all the passengers waiting for permission to board. He was there too, hidden in the crowd, as mesmerised as anyone, yet still able to raise a lens and capture that moment before he disappeared.

Even though she knew who it was, even if she knew the details, still the picture had an amazing effect - uplifting, filled with happiness, radiating love.

As she turned to face the photographer's wife, tears streaming down her joyful cheeks, she heard a truth she never knew.

"You changed his life. You changed so many lives. Something happened on that boat and a wave of love flowed out into the world. Come, follow me."

And she followed the photographer's wife down a long corridor, and a series of perfectly lit black and white portraits, each capturing a moment in the life of someone touched by love.

They sat together drinking tea in a large studio room, lit by a wall of windows that opened out onto the park. It was part lounge, part gallery, sofas arranged in a square around low tables, furniture arranged such that each sofa offered a place from which to gaze at images of beauty and peace and love. And as she gazed, gently weeping, the photographer's wife spoke to her.

"My husband was a beautiful man - pure and kind and good. We went to school together and I loved him from the moment we met. And from that first moment I watched him change the world around him through small acts of kindness and love.

"As we grew up, he thought he could bring peace to the world by revealing the truth as he saw it. And he revealed that truth through his words and the images he collected as he travelled.

"He travelled to war zones, hoping to create a wave of awareness that would stop the human horror. But we began to pay a price. Each time he returned, he returned with a little less of himself, a little less able to love, a little less able to be loved. And finally, he didn't return.

"I don't know how old Imad was when he met my husband - probably no more than a teenager, yet he dragged him from where he fell and stayed with him as he died. My husband wrote a letter, a beautiful letter to send back to me, knowing he was dying, knowing I would never see him again.

"My husband asked Imad to take a picture of him before he died and Imad captured everything I loved. I'll show it to you later. Imad returned with help to the place where my husband died. They removed his body and buried him well, marking a grave for me to visit and say goodbye.

"That was the only time we met, and Imad told me by my husband's grave, that he would continue his work and record the truth and show the world. I agreed to sell his photographs if I could. And I could. Something deep was exchanged that night and his photographs were as easy to sell as my husband's.

"And that's how we continued. Imad sent his films and I sold them through my husband's agent, cabling the money to Imad's account. I never looked at any of them.

"I had seen enough suffering and I was no longer convinced that revealing the truth could make a difference.

"Then he met you, and everything changed. The technician at the printers found that photograph of you at the end of a roll and called me to the lab. From then on, Imad only ever sent portraits. I couldn't sell them but I cabled the money anyway - I had enough for it to make no difference to me.

"I printed and framed the portraits as they came. In all I received nine rolls, and each shot was as extraordinary as the last. I printed and framed every one and stored them here. And then there were no more rolls. And then there was no more account and the money I sent was returned.

"All these years I have waited. All these years I have kept this wing of our apartment as a shrine to my dead husband. All these years I have kept this collection hidden. Until this year, when I suddenly let go of the past and created this gallery, watching as these photographs changed the lives of everyone who saw them. Come, let me show you my husband."

She followed the photographer's wife back to the entrance, into the other wing of the apartment, into her bedroom, to stand in front of the portrait of her husband. And she stood transfixed, her thinking stopped, her sense of self flowing like love through a mind freed of all thoughts, a body freed of all tensions.

"I don't understand. Imad said they met in a war zone, in a bomb crater. Imad said they spent the night together - a night of shelling and shooting. He said your husband helped him through that night, helped him to keep his soul. Imad said your husband was shot by a sniper. But you said Imad took this photograph as your husband was dying. I don't understand. He's clean. He's smiling. He's beautiful. His image fills my heart with hope, with love, with happiness."

"That's true. But this is not how my husband looked, this is how my husband was. This is the effect he had, not the way he appeared. This is how I remember him, how everybody remembered him."

"But how can that be. How could he do that."

"I don't know how he did it. But I do know why. He did it because of you. As you say, my husband helped Imad keep his soul and, because of that, he vowed to continue my husband's work. But my husband was already lost. In the end all he could see was violence and sadness. He forgot that it was his love that changed the world and he sacrificed his love for truth. But as he was dying, he remembered himself and that is when Imad took that picture.

"Imad didn't understand until he met you. Your love helped him remember himself, and he carried that love out into the world.

"There is one more photograph I haven't showed you yet."

She led her to another room, a small room that opened from the lounge, simply decorated, simply lit, with one chair, one photograph.

She sat and gazed at the photograph of her and Imad, young, beautiful, happy, in love, hand in hand, standing on the jetty on Paros, watching the ferry leave.

Printed in Great Britain
by Amazon

75970670R10085